Beautiful Jaded Butterflies

Sometimes love is nothing but a game of chess.

Book Two in the Mated Fortune Series

J.P. Mooney

DEDICATION

Goddesses of all dimensions. May you express your passion, sexuality and indulge in worldly pleasures. Live your truth.

CONTENTS

Chapter One

Isabella

It had been one year since my life took a turn for the worse. At first, it felt as though I was living in a dream. Even when I thought that maybe I had always lived that way, the ordeal with my mother, moving to London without guidance in an attempt to start fresh, I felt that I had finally settled into the best life I worked so hard to make for myself. Not a lot changed after the debacle with Ryan. The only thing that I thought had changed was the way I conducted business with my clients. I decided that a woman like me in such a business couldn't be too careful. So, I decided to sell my apartment and move. You may be slightly confused as to who I am. If you are not remotely familiar with my story, I suggest you read all about my fabulous city adventures in *Isabella, Book One* in the *Mated Fortune* series. I am Isabella. Most would conclude that I'm an escort, although I detest this word. I am a brilliant woman who spends time with affluent men for a lavish lifestyle. At this point in life, I have accumulated so much money that I merely just spend time with these men for a high-class level of leisure.

In the early years of my adult life, I developed a stone heart that no man could penetrate. And then I fucked up by sleeping with a man named Andrew, accidentally killed him and fell in love with his brother who turned out to be involved in a blackmailing game that nearly ruined my life. His name was Ryan. That was before I found out he was conspiring with Andrew's friend and business associate, John to make mine and Frank's life a living hell. Poor Frank. He's my best friend, and we had grown closer throughout the situation, but I fucked up again. I let my anger take control, and I killed both

John and Ryan. I couldn't stand dragging him down with me into the mess of my life, so I told him to keep a distance.

One thing is for sure. I thought I had no heart before, which worked incredibly well for when I conducted business with clients. Shortly after the murders, I considered ending my own life. As I stood on that bridge and glared down at the murky water, I realised that I wasn't done. Sure, the situation was terrible. However, I also had some fabulous memories. I was beautiful, rich and cunning but since then, I decided to be beautiful, rich and damn right savage. Andrew, John and Ryan were gone, along with the memories of my self-indulgent pitiful days. It was time to have some fun. I decided to sell my apartment and bought a new one more east of the city. It had been eight months since I had seen Frank. Sure, we messaged each other here, and there, however, I thought that a reunion was due. We decided to have a change of scene and meet for dinner and drinks in Shoreditch. The mid-July air was stuffy, and the rush hour commuters were sparse for a Friday in the Eastend. The sun was just beginning to set, and my shoes sparkled as I climbed out of my cab. The street was buzzing, women and men of all ages with unsatiated taste in fashion paraded along the pavement, some stood in groups sipping beers and leaning against the colourful walls.

I found the name of the restaurant and made my way up the steps to the foyer. *Choux*. It looked precisely like somewhere Frank would choose. Gold trimmings and furnishing all around while the diamante chandelier hung proudly on the ceiling. The host showed me to the table, and as I followed behind, my heart skipped a beat when I saw Frank sitting elegantly at the table in the far corner. His hair had changed, his muscles were larger and taut, and his face still chiselled to perfection. I was elated. The hostess set our menus on the table as Frank stood up to greet me. We stared at each other for a moment and without hesitation, reached into an embrace that felt familiar and safe. Our friendship hadn't started on trust although we had a lot of fun together. Nonetheless, we grew into it. We sat down, and I couldn't help but continuously glance at him excitedly and giggling like a child. We ordered wine and appetisers, which arrived quickly.

"Omg, Izzy! What the hell happened? I know you said it was taken care of, but I keep looking at the news, browsing forums and all corners of the web and aside from the mention eleven months ago, there's nothing." He said expectantly.

"I know. To be quite honest I don't know what the fuck is going on anymore and I'm just hoping that I can put it all behind me, behind us. What I do know is that although Ryan came across as the nice guy in this situation, or at least I thought he was, he knew everything and was trying to convince me not to get rid of John. But then I asked myself, could I really trust him? If he knew about the blackmailing and helped Juliana to take down his own brother, imagine what else he could do. Playing his own games and pitting people against each other. Besides, he knew too much about the situation, about you and me. I couldn't let him ruin us."

Frank listened intently. I knew he understood that I had to do it, and as always, he never judged. We lived a very dark life, and we were sitting in the deepest part of oblivion. We had to move forward.

"So, what now?" He searched my face for hope.

"Well, I have enough money in savings, but I still see clients however, I am extremely cautious. I don't bring them home. I sold the apartment and bought a new one which you're more than welcomed to crash in tonight. I want us to look forward to life again. Things won't be the same because we are not the same people, we're more experienced now." I grinned.

"You're right. And I'm more beautiful now, so fuck it. Live the high life until the end." We clinked our glasses and sipped our drinks.

The night was just as fabulous as our previous nights out in the city. Only this time, we had grown in confidence and strength. When dinner finished, we took a cab back to my new home, which was only a ten minutes' drive down the road. I opted for a 5th-floor apartment with a white and gold minimalistic décor. The change of scheme was needed to signify a fresh start, and it was also easy to leave bare and still look chic. I didn't want to fill the space with too many furniture in case I needed to leave in a hurry. I didn't tell Frank this. He was too busy twirling around the room and swooning.

"Alright, miss fancy. I see you." We giggled.

The evening flew by quickly, and I was content with the lightness of our friendship. He agreed to crash on my sofa after we had drunk two bottles of prosecco. As

I showered and nursed myself into bed, I extended thoughts of gratitude to Frank and fell asleep with a smile stretched across my face.

Chapter Two

Frank

I was hesitant to meet her, but one thing is for sure, I couldn't say no to Isabella. As we sat and talked throughout dinner, I realised that not only did I miss her like crazy, I missed the part of my character that manifested when I was with her, the carefree sparkle that enveloped my personality. Nothing had changed for me except love. I met Mathew when John was blackmailing myself and Isabella. John had pulled me so deep into his games that at one point, it caused a fracture between Isabella and me. She lost her temper, and rightfully so that I binged on sugary cocktails in a club and ended up bringing Mathew back to my apartment. However, it was more Mathew who brought me back to my apartment as I blacked out. We dated for a while, and it eventually blossomed into something real. This relationship was more concrete than any affair I had indulged in my lifetime, and it was proving to keep my playboy mode in check for the foreseeable future. I stirred and caught myself as I nearly fell off Isabella's sofa. My eyes were pulsing in their sockets, and my head felt heavy as I tried to lift it off the pillow to look around the room. Memories of the night before flashed through me, and I remembered that I crashed in Isabella's new home. The sun hadn't risen yet; however, the faint glow from the lamp in the corner was enough to reassure and put me as ease. I dozily made my way to the kitchen and poured myself a glass of water as the buzzing sound of the fridge mocked my stance. The coolness soothed my throat and my mind. I rummaged in the fridge for a snack and settled for a pot of organic yoghurt and some grapes. I retired back to the sofa to eat and waited for the sunrise before I woke up Isabella. Just as I decided to stand and walk to her room, the door opened. She emerged wearing nothing but a satin robe that openly flowed behind her. My eyes grew wide as I took in her beauty. Her brown skin was smooth and supple, her breasts were plump and her black hair, although I preferred it curly was now straight and highlighted with brown streaks that gave her an edge.

"What? She grinned as she tied it close.

"Your body is, wow. Have you been working out harder?"

She nodded as she walked over and touched my arms, pressing deep into my muscles.

"Erm excuse your arms. We would make a killer couple." We both giggled because it felt right.

We decided to have a proper breakfast before I departed, which consisted of vegetarian sausages, scrambled eggs, beans and fresh fruits. She wasn't a vegan although she had always watched her diet, Isabella announced that she was trying to eat less meat to improve her mental clarity. If she wasn't giving up martinis and bourbons, I was okay with whatever path she chose. I thanked her for breakfast and made my way home feeling euphoric. I took a cab back home to Charing Cross. Just as Isabella, I contemplated finding a new apartment more west of the city, however, I didn't want to move further away from my job on the south bank and certainly was not entertaining the idea of working in another gallery. My hosting skills significantly matched my current employer, and the team loved me. When I arrived home, Mathew was busy cooking brunch. The notes of oregano, olive oil and the melodic tone of his music floated with me to the kitchen.

"You're in a good mood." I kissed him and leaned on the counter next to where he stood.

"I missed you. And I thought you may have eaten breakfast at Isabella's but wasn't sure how substantial it was so I'm making sweet potato frittata."

"I have eaten, but this brunch sounds too delicious to pass on. Perks of having a chef boyfriend". I caught myself noticing that I had never called him my boyfriend out loud. It felt nice.

I walked to the hallway and checked the table for the post. I flicked through the small batch, looking for something interesting. Leaflets, brochures, bank statements and a small pink envelope with my name and address handwritten, but there were no stamps which meant someone had hand delivered. I assumed it was a card from the neighbour I helped with their shopping a few weeks prior when they had broken their leg. The envelope had only a small card inside and a message.

Please stay away from her or go down with her—your choice.

My body froze as my heart flung itself between the walls of my chest. I had no idea who's handwriting it was, but I did know for sure that they were talking about Isabella. In my frozen state, I heard Mathew's voice fading in the distance. Sweat started to cascade from my forehead, and my fingers were shaking. There was no way that I could tell Mathew about all of this. He knew that Isabella and I played on a little naughty side of life, but he didn't know to what extent.

"You okay?" Mathew's voice snapped me back to the room. I quickly shoved the card in my pocket and smiled.

"Err yeah, just thought I had a déjà vu. Let's eat." I kissed him and walked to the kitchen.

I couldn't remember what we spoke about over brunch with the note burning a hole in my pocket. I smiled and tried to be my usual self, yet, I had to admit that I was shit scared. I had tried to move on after the Andrew, Ryan and John situation, and the last thing I needed was more trouble. At one point, I thought that perhaps I was overthinking it. But given how our lives spiralled out of control over the last year it was unlikely that a bored teenager decided to pick Isabella and me as the centrepiece of their prank. For sure, I didn't know if this note was related to any previous troubles, but I wasn't taking any chances. I messaged Isabella, and she called right away. She sounded oddly calm on the phone but considering the ordeal she had been through, literally killing three people and getting away with it, I wasn't surprised. We decided to meet at her place after I finished work and until then I just had to go on living my life as it were.

Chapter Three

Isabella

I couldn't lie and say that I wasn't concerned in the slightest because I was. Most of the people I knew who were involved in the game was now dead except for Juliana. Although Ryan didn't mention if she knew anything about Andrew's blackmailing, I couldn't leave this situation up to faith. By the tone of the note that was sent to Frank, whoever sent it had plans to take me down. Whether that meant plans to send me to prison, kill me or send my arse home with a beating, I wasn't taking any chances. It was still early in the day, so I asked Frank to come over after he finished his shift. In the meantime, I decided to do some online research by looking for Juliana's social media profiles. It wasn't difficult to find her. Just like many people, she also kept her profiles public and posted holiday pictures for the world to see and boost her ego. I would be lying if I said I was impressed. Nothing on her profiles indicated that she was up to anything malicious. If anything, she looked like she had swiftly moved on from the burdens of her past holidays in Greece, Mexico and Paris. I couldn't fault her for taking control and rearranging her life. Boredom soon enough engulfed me, so I decided it was time to go for a run.

I changed in my running kit, laced up my trainers, slathered sunscreen on my face and made my way to the park. The afternoon heat just began to rise, and the dog walkers were dispersed into small groups ready to begin their adventures at the entrance of the park. I took in a deep breath and began my laps, reaching for the furthest side of the park. I must've gotten lost in my music because I wandered off the path and bumped into a mysterious man. My headphone fell out of my ear, and a frisson crept through my spine. I turned around to apologise, but by the time I did, he had already disappeared. That feeling stayed with me all day, and I was struggling to cope with the idea that the cycle of my life may have started again. I made a vow to be as healthy as I could physically, mentally and spiritually, and part of my daily routine was a meditating ritual. After I showered and replenished my stomach with a salad, I decided to light some candles to set my intention for meditation. I positioned myself on the floor and allowed my mind to drift into darkness. Frank arrived just as I finished eating dinner. He looked mildly sweaty and spaced out.

"Are you alright?" I asked sceptically.

"I can't believe this is happening again."

He slumped on the sofa and rubbed his temple. I wanted to lie to comfort him. The last thing I wanted was for anything to push Frank over the edge.

"I know. Look I don't know who this could be for sure, but there's only one person alive in all this. Juliana." He shot me a look. "There's not a lot we can do for the moment. Just be careful and keep your head down."

I told him that I had looked up Juliana's socials and will continue to keep track to find anything suspicious although, she had been living her best life. We decided to do what we did best mostly since we hadn't seen each other in a while. Frank always looked put together and polished that he didn't even have to change clothes for the club. The cab dropped us outside *Bar Hugh,* which was up and coming on the edge of Shoreditch. It was just after 9 p.m. and the queue was beginning to congest with attitudes. The bouncer checked our IDs and ushered us in where we made our direct route to the bar.

"Two gin and tonics good sir!" Frank flirted with the bartender who was very much loving the attention. We sipped our drinks as we asked the hostess if we could pay for a private booth since it was still quiet. To our luck, she agreed and let us cocoon in our velvet corner.

"Just like the good old days."

"Gosh, it's only been a few months." I smiled.

I noticed that Frank was making eyes with the bartender as the beat of the music increased its pace.

"So, how's Mathew?" I tried to divert his attention in hopes of preventing him from doing something he may regret, however, we both knew that Frank just did whatever the hell he wanted.

"Boring! He cooks, he cleans and works out which is the perfect qualities in a relationship but fucking hell I'm bored. I wake up, and he's there. I get home from work, and he's still there. It's a bit much sometimes." He sipped his drink.

"I hear you, but still it must be nice to have a companion." I smiled. Frank wasn't having any of it. He shrugged and looked over at the bar.

"Calm down, babe. I'm only browsing."

15

I smiled and politely excused myself for the bathroom. Making my way down the stairs past the cloakroom, I gave a gentle smile to the attendant as I noticed a presence lurking in the dark corner of the corridor. I didn't stop to look, but I quickened my pace to the ladies. I found an empty cubicle on the far end to use. I thought I didn't need to use the bathroom; however, something in that corridor gave me the creeps, and I was reluctant to go back outside on my own. I fumbled through my bag for my phone and messaged Frank to meet me by the cloakroom. Just as I sent the message, the door opened, and the person slowly walked to the sinks. It sounds ridiculous, but my heart began to race with my instincts. I decided that whoever was messing with me would know exactly who it was they were messing with. I was in no mood for nobody's bullshit. I took a deep breath and lunged the cubicle door open to surprise the creep, but there was nobody there. Confused, I checked in all the cubicles to find them empty. I quickly washed my hand and made my way back to the bar. Frank startled me when I opened the door to leave as he caught his chest with his hand.

"For fucks sakes. You've had one gin you can't be drunk already. What's going on?" He howled.

We walked back to the booth, and I told him about the mysterious presence on my way to the bathroom. He nervously laughed it off although, I knew Frank was more concerned than he was letting on. It was time to take our minds off the eerie activities and lose ourselves into a dance. We did just that until 1 a.m. when we both took a cab home.

My phone pinged a message from Frank that prompted me to get out of bed.

Shit. Call me.

Confused, I called him immediately.

"What's wrong? Are you okay?" My heart began to race.

"I slept with the bartender from last night. Mathew thinks I'm at yours." He didn't even have to ask. Frank knew that I would always have his back.

"Yes, you were at mine. We will talk about it the next time we meet." I reassured him before we said goodbye.

I knew that most people would frown and judge our choices, but I understood Frank's character, and he did mine. A part of me knew that he would end up sleeping with the bartender from *Bar Hugh* yet, I also hoped that he would've spared Mathew the heartbreak. As I moved around the kitchen making brunch, a tingle worked up and down my spine when I remembered the weird phenomena from the night before. As I walked through it, I realised it was the same feeling I had when I bumped into the mysterious person in the park. I decided to check my socials as I ate brunch on the sofa. I scrolled through my blog as usual and halted when I received a message request from a profile I didn't recognise. For sure I knew that it couldn't have been Juliana considering her intelligent background in property management unless she was bored enough to take time out of her day to fuck around without the use of a dictionary or thesaurus.

Rozes r red
Violets r blu
John n Ange r dead
Babes u r 2.

Rage surged through my body as I flung my phone on the sofa. My heart was beating for a release, and a thirst for violence filled my throat. My thoughts were chaotic, and my vision was blurred. I needed to calm down. A moment passed when I gained clarity. I checked through the profile, but there were no photos or information posted. I sent Frank the screenshot of the message with the profile name.

Wtf?! I'll get the boys to track and scan the profile.

I stared blankly at my phone since I didn't know Frank had such capacity.

They'll find out who it is. Come to the apartment for dinner.

I trusted that if anyone could figure out who was behind this, it would be Frank's guys. The mystery guys that packed and transported Andrew's body out of my living room a year ago. I spent most of my day trying to not obsess over the direct message. What messed with me the most was that it seemed whoever was messing with me acted like they didn't know who I was. If they did, they would know that I had no qualms to deal with whatever issues they had with me head-on in the best way I knew. I spent minutes that turned into hours sitting in silence. Eventually, I knew that I needed something to take the edge off my anxiety. I booked a cab to Frank's apartment and made sure the driver took the quickest route to Charing Cross. As we drove down the back streets, I saw couples walking gallantly, workers leaning on the side of office buildings taking advantage of their smoke breaks and thought how lovely it would be if life were this simple. And then I thought about my beautiful apartment and the holidays I've taken knowing that I would not have traded it for anything.

I arrived at Frank's apartment at about 6 p.m. and took a deep breath before I rang the bell.

"Come in. It's open!"

I slowly made my way down the hallway where the smell of Mathew's cooking seduced my stomach. I was hungry. Mathew walked over just as he saw and kissed my cheeks.

"Gorgeous. Good to see you, darling, Frank is plodding around in the bedroom. I'll call out when dinner is ready."

"Thanks, Mathew." I grinned. As I made my way to their bedroom, I tried to bury whatever guilt I felt for knowing that Frank cheated on him. After all, Frank is my best friend first and foremost, and they are both adults.

I walked in the bedroom and saw Frank sitting on the bed looking a bit spaced out. I crawled on the other side to him.

"I got your message. I thought I'd get started on this vape while I waited for you to counsel me." He passed the vape to me, and I inhaled the herby goodness.

"I would if I were you too. Gosh, I've done nothing productive today yet I'm so stressed and exhausted because of that message. Do you have any update on a lead?" I took another inhale and enjoyed the elevated feeling as the heavy fog lifted off my head.

"Not yet, they work quickly, so tomorrow morning at the latest." We froze in silence for a moment.

"I fucked it, Izzy. I'm such a selfish prick. I have no right to burden this on Mathew in hopes that he'll forgive me. I have to break up with him." He closed his eyes and swallowed hard. I really felt bad for him. I knew he loved Mathew and how much Mathew loved him. However, Frank had commitment issues, and that was just the plain truth.

"You have to do what is best for you, babe." I placed my hand on his.

Minutes later, Mathew called us out for dinner. The table was set elegantly, and he chose an excellent brand of wine. We took our places as Mathew served his duck confit, salmon en croute and dauphinoise potato. I was trying to consume less meat, however, considering it was a Wednesday and I was high, I didn't care. Dinner was delicious, and my stomach was satiated. The conversation carried on as usual; however, I sensed that Frank was floating in his mind, which could potentially be apparent to Mathew. The last thing I wanted to experience was their relationship breaking down at that moment. He noticed my gaze on him and relaxed his shoulders.

"Is everything okay babe? You seem a little off." Mathew asked.

"I cheated on you." Frank said as he turned and extended a cold look straight at Mathew. The air froze between us and the heavy rumble in my stomach sobered me faster than a cold shower. Nothing was said for a moment, and I felt lightheaded. I liked Mathew, and he didn't deserve this humiliation.

"I'm going to leave. I'm so sorry, thank you for dinner." I said as I quickly shimmied my way out, stumbling over as I grabbed my bag.

My exit was a blur, and my mind started to clear when I arrived home. I felt so guilty for not trying harder to divert Frank's attention from that night, and it all felt too real being in Mathew's presence. I felt the urge to throw up.

Chapter Four

Frank

I had convinced myself that I wasn't going to tell Mathew about my indiscretion, that I would let him go unafflicted and unburdened. Sitting there with him and Izzy brewed incredible guilt that I didn't think I was capable of feeling. I didn't want to lose him, but I owed him honesty.

"What the fuck are you talking about?" He spat.

"The other night I went out with Izzy, I slept with the bartender. I'm sorry. It was just seeing you here all the time; it scared me. I'm sorry. I love you."

"And the entire time you both sat here eating the food that I cooked. Smiling and pretending." He stood up and attempted to clear the table.

"Babe, please. I'm sorry. I'm being honest."

"Well, since we're being honest. You're a spoilt brat with bullshit excuses who throw people away as soon as you're bored. You're not better than me, Frank. I deserve better, and I'm leaving."

He pushed past me and made his way to the bedroom and started packing his clothes. I wanted to cry, but I didn't want to make this more painful.

"Baby, please. Stay at least until tomorrow morning. It's getting late, where are you going to go?"

"I have plenty of people who care about me. I'll be back to collect the rest of my things." He slammed the door as he left.

A stillness settled in the apartment, and I felt uncomfortable. I didn't want to deal with this, and I thought of it as no love loss. I took my phone and called a friend. My doorbell rang thirty minutes later, and the handsome man that appeared in my hallway was enough to get me excited.

"Lars, you made it."

"Nice to see you again." He smiled.

We walked to the kitchen, where I poured us a drink. Then we retired in the living room for a chat.

"Nice place."

I looked around and nodded in agreement. I had already cleaned up from the disastrous dinner. It was as though nothing had happened. We made small talk, and all I could think about was how badly I wanted to repeat the session we had the night we met at *Bar Hugh*. Lars was obviously thinking about the same thing because he leaned in and kissed me hard. My mouth parted open as our tongues entwined with excitement. We fucked a few times throughout the night, my energy was fuelled by the Patron tequila he brought with him. Morning arrived, and my body ached like it had been run over by a lorry. I pulled myself out of bed and headed to the kitchen for some coffee. The clock pinged 8 a.m. when I heard the front door open. I froze in shame when Mathew walked through the kitchen. We stood in silence and looked at each other for a moment when Lars shouted from the bedroom.

"Is the coffee on sexy?" I cringed as his voice echoed around the apartment.

"What the fuck!" Mathew trailed his way to the bedroom where the door was wide open, displaying Lars, spread naked on the bed. My mouth dropped open at the sight of them both.

"Babe, it didn't mean anything."

Mathew walked around the house, grabbing the rest of his things, packing them into cardboard boxes.

"You're unbelievable. I came here thinking that maybe there's a part of me that could work through this with you. You couldn't even keep your dick tucked in your trousers long enough to reflect on us. And the guy is here, still rolling around in my bed, so I think that shows that it does mean something."

Lars walked over, thankfully dressed in his clothes from the night before. His face was calm and empathetic.

"Don't worry bro. I'm not mad at you. He's all yours." Mathew spat as he placed cardboard boxes on the trolley he left in the hallway and walked out.

Lars walked to the kitchen, poured us some coffee and heated some croissants for breakfast. I opened a small box that resided under the coffee table and rolled myself a joint. Yes, it was early, and I rarely did this, but it was an exceptional occasion. I took a draw and passed it to Lars to oblige and share my pain. We scoffed breakfast and had a long talk about the situation. Lars understood that the idea of us being in a relationship was redundant.

"I know it hurts you deep down, so you try to soothe it with sex, but eventually you need to admit that you fucked up. Choose to work through it and make it up to him or move on, making better choices." He said as he puffed out the smoke.

I smoked and pondered on his words long after Lars left. With each inhale, I sunk deeper into my thoughts and the sofa. Suddenly, the front door opened, and I jumped with adrenaline, hoping it was Mathew.

"Nope, just me!" Izzy spoke as she kicked off her shoes and walked to the living room.

"You gave me a key for emergencies and Mathew called to give me a piece of his mind this morning, so I thought if this isn't an emergency then what is." She giggled as she climbed on the sofa and nestled herself in my arms.

We talked about Mathew for the entire day. For the first time in a long time, I felt like shit for hurting someone, and it was because I cared about him. We smoked, drank tequila and ordered pizza. Then I received a call from one of my boys that I took on speakerphone.

"I traced the IP to an address. It's a hotel down Aldwych. They were cautious about using a computer from there. The backend of this account is plain. Tell your girl to leave the line of communication open so I can check for trends." He hung up.

"Wow, he's all about doing his job with no small talk." Izzy said.

"Yes, he is. You heard what he said. It could be anyone at this point, so let the games begin."

The evening eventually came, and we decided to head out for a walk in Aldwych, which wasn't far from my apartment. With the new information, we accepted that it was easier for the person to hand-deliver the note because they knew that my apartment was quite close and that again, I would end up being the easy target. The high had subsided, and I was happy to put Mathew at the back of my mind for a while. Izzy and I decided to have a drink at a quaint bar across the road from the hotel. We parked ourselves in a hidden corner by the window where we could see the hustle and bustle of the hotel entrance. We nursed our drinks for thirty minutes when Izzy decided to respond to the messenger on her social.

Boo! I see you, and now you're dead too. :)

Of course, this was bullshit. We had no substantial knowledge of the creep to start making threats, however, considering they wanted to start a game of cat and mouse, we thought it would be a good idea to push forward and flush them out. Within minutes of sending the message, Isabella's phone rang. She picked up after a few rings and didn't say a word. The person didn't say a word either as I took my gaze around the bar to see if they were there. Just as I turned my head to look at the entrance of the hotel, I saw someone wearing a hood, leaning against the wall and holding their phone to their ear. I nudged Izzy to look, and she hung up the call.

"It has to be them; I can just feel it." I said with adrenaline.

"No, they can't be that careless. They must've called on a burner. Let me redial the number."

She called the number as our eyes remained glued on the person lingering outside the hotel. They starred at their phone as it rang and walked inside the shop next door to the hotel. I grabbed Isabella's arm as I sprung towards the door. We crossed the road and approached the shop quickly and carefully, while my heart drummed inside my chest. The alcoholic drinks stirred and fuelled my adrenaline as my feet pushed the pace to reach the pavement on the other side of the road. Since Isabella had changed her hair to become less recognisable, she thought it would be better if she wandered past the shop for a quick look. Just as she was about to creep in for a closer look, the hooded person abruptly walked out of the shop to the hotel entrance. We followed quietly and slowly behind with our visions locked onto them. The hooded person walked to the concierge made small talk and headed for the hotel bar. Isabella followed. I grabbed her arm as I was hesitant to get closer.

"We have to get a closer look to see who it is Frank." She pleaded.

"I don't want to sink deep into this hole. This person could be dangerous."

"More dangerous than us?" She smirked.

She had a point. Although I wasn't a murderer, I indeed was guilty by association. Isabella walked to the concierge and made small talk while pretending to be a guest at the hotel. He was a charming man in a navy-blue suit who had no issue obliging her conversation while I lurked at the entrance of the bar to keep my eyes on the hooded person. The person ordered a whisky, sipped it neat at the bar while checking their phone. Carefully, trying to not draw attention to myself, I continued to try and catch a glimpse of their face. I looked over at Isabella, who was busy smiling in conversation with the concierge. My heart pounded when I noticed the hooded person making their way out of the bar. I trotted to Izzy and told her to go in the ladies and wait for my text. She seamlessly excused herself and did as I asked and with a stroke of sudden luck, the concierge guy went outside to greet new arrivals. I hid in the furthest corner of the lobby that I could find while tracing my eyes on the hooded person, quite astonished that they had the nerve to parade around the hotel with their hood on. They made their way to the lift, and I watched the numbers stop on the 10th floor, assuming it was where they stayed. The lift didn't stop at other floors and quickly pressed the call button to check if it went further up which it didn't. This gave us a lead. I messaged Isabella to wait for me in the shop next door as I climbed the stairs to the 10th

floor while my mind swayed into dark memories from a few months before. My legs hated me as I reached the 10th floor but considering I hadn't been to the gym in a while, I thought a quick workout was due and didn't complain. The room door next to the staircase swung open as I exited, sending a wave of panic through me. Fortunately for me, it was the hotel attendant retrieving fresh linen from her trolley.

"Excuse me, madam, I wonder if you could help me." I said with the most charming, inviting smile that pushed her on the edge of a blush.

"Yes, do you need your room changed urgently?"

"No that's okay, thank you. The thing is, I booked a room downstairs because I suspect my girlfriend has been meeting another man here. I thought I saw them walking up here together. Have you perhaps seen them?" I was struggling to hold in my laugh as the attendant's eyes grew wide with shock as she rubbed my arm with empathy.

"Oh, my darling, that's terrible."

"I know, I was devastated when I found the text messages and pictures, she had sent him, but I had to see it for myself before I make the right decisions for our children." Got her!

"What do they look like?"

"My girlfriend is blonde and tall. The man, I couldn't see. He had a blue hood on." I bit my lip and forced moisture to my eyes.

"Ah! I didn't see a tall blonde woman. But a man in a blue hood went in there." She pointed to the furthest room at the end of the corridor, number 17. I quickly ended the conversation and thanked her with a twenty pounds note for her knowledge. I waited until she entered her next room, pretending to pluck up the courage to confront my imaginary cheating girlfriend. Yes, I felt terrible for lying, but I knew it was necessary. I made my exit back down the stairs and met Izzy in the shop next door.

"Where the fuck have you been?!" She said mid-chew as she set her sandwich on the plate. I took a large bite and decided to finish it since I was instantly famished.

"Long story short, I found out that the person we saw booked room 17 on the 10th floor of the hotel. The room attendant confirmed this, so it's worth something.

We looked at each other and sighed with exhaustion realising that it was now too far past dinner time. We decided to head back to my apartment to regroup. As we walked through the door, the memory of the day that lead up to the last few hours tumbled and stressed on my shoulders. The thought of Mathew had seeped out of my mind, and now it all came rushing back. We ate our leftover pizzas, hit the vape until we crashed out on the sofa.

Chapter Five

Isabella

Memories of the previous day's revelation caused a stir in my stomach as I awoke from Frank's sofa with a dry mouth and a mental fog. I looked over to see Frank still sound asleep as I walked to the kitchen to make breakfast. My heart ached for Frank and Mathew. A part of me still hoped that they would work things out, but they both needed time to heal. I whipped up a quick breakfast with strong coffee to set us up for the day. Frank walked in the kitchen with nothing but his pyjama bottoms on. The muscles on his core almost killed my eyes.

"Good morning to you too." He smirked.

"You've never announced when you're hitting the gym, and somehow, your body is just, stunning!" My eyes were locked on his chest.

"Oh, stop it." He playfully said.

We ate our breakfast and chatted about our plans for the rest of the day. Frank had to go to work, and I had a client booked at lunchtime. I had a quick refreshing shower and headed home. I arrived home at 11 a.m., which was enough time to exercise and have a proper shower before meeting my client at 1 p.m. I practised my yoga poses and plunged myself in an indulgent bath as I began the process of getting ready. It wasn't unusual to have clients book meetings for lunch since some of them were in the city for a short time. At 1 p.m. I walked inside the beautiful lobby of the *Grand Hotel Victoria* situated in Westminster. The host greeted and guided me to my client, who booked a booth in the furthest corner of the restaurant.

"Patrick, it's lovely to see you again."

"You too, Izzy. You look gorgeous as always."

Patrick was a recurring client whom I generally enjoyed being in his presence. In the past, I rarely booked new clients if my current network didn't recommend them; however, now I was even more careful to ensure I kept my list exclusive. We chatted for a while and enjoyed a delicious meal paired with the finest wine. An hour later, we were reclined naked on his bed in the hotel room he had booked.

"You seem distant today, is everything okay?"

One of my rules was never to discuss my issues with my client, but I was distant as the weight of having a stalker hung over my head. I needed to talk to someone aside from Frank.

"My sister had started receiving odd messages on her socials. The police can't do anything about it because it's anonymous, so I'm trying to help her find out who it is."

"Oh my, that's awful. I don't know how to help except what I would do is perhaps narrow down everyone she may have pissed off or had unfinished business with then take it from there."

As soon as Patrick mentioned 'unfinished business' a biochemical alarm lit inside me. The entire time I was keeping an eye on Juliana and thinking that perhaps she was bored enough to do this to me when in fact we only had one lunch together and she knew nothing about me. Except Ryan mentioned that she was quite close to him, so she could've been doing this for revenge. I had a shower, got dressed and wished Patrick a safe flight as I left the hotel and headed straight to see Frank at work. The cab driver glared at me through his rear-view mirror as I tried to focus my mind on the information circulating in my head. The cab stopped on the main road as I made my way along the river to Frank's gallery. Slight anxiety sizzled in my stomach as I rarely visited Frank at work in case, I bumped into one of my clients. I wasn't scared of their reaction as they were sophisticated people. However, I refused to voluntarily put myself in the presence of their wives or girlfriends. That's the type of drama I was allergic to. I messaged Frank to meet me at the terrace bar, where I promptly ordered myself a bourbon.

"Izzy, what's the matter?" He said as he greeted me with urgency.

"It's Ryan." I didn't want it to be true. The feelings I buried deep in my subconscious rushed to the surface. I didn't have enough evidence to prove that it was him, but my intuition was never wrong.

"What, how do you know?"

"I was with a client today, and I vaguely mentioned the situation but pretended it was my sister. And he said that the first thing he would do is narrow down everyone he had unfinished business with or may have pissed off."

"I'm not following." Frank said hesitantly.

"I've checked everywhere, Frank. There's nothing online indicating that Ryan's body was found. I know the hotel didn't want anything leaked in the press, but I've been digging and found nothing. Not even Juliana had posted anything about losing him. And that message I received, it mentioned that John and Andrew are dead but why not also mention Ryan? It would make sense for him to live in a hotel too." My mind was spinning. A sudden panic crept up and down my spine with the realisation that Ryan was seeking revenge. I didn't want to go home and do nothing.

"Okay, calm down. We'll get to the bottom of this. Take a deep breath and order another drink. I'll come back after I finish my shift."

I ordered another bourbon and sat near the window where I could keep my eyes on the entrance. I had always felt guilty for overdosing or in this case, attempting to overdose Ryan. As much as I didn't want to admit it, my heart fluttered with the memories of our time together and the idea that we could have had something extraordinary in a normal situation. An hour later, I saw that Frank had changed into his casual outfit as he took a seat facing me. We decided it would be better for him to sleepover at my apartment as we needed to figure out our next steps. We arrived home just before dinner time. Frank ordered takeaways from the local Italian restaurant while I poured and sipped another bourbon.

"Right. I'm going to see if one of the guys can help figure this shit out by hacking into the hotel's CCTV to see if we can get a view of the hooded person."

My stomach was in a knotted mess. For sure, I wanted confirmation, but I was also afraid of what I would have to do if it revealed that it was Ryan. It didn't take long for Frank to receive a reply.

"Are you ready?" He asked with hesitation.

"How much are you paying these people?"

"Enough for them to not ask questions. Stop procrastinating. Let's do this."

We both held our breaths as the picture loaded on his phone screen. The image was quite dark, and the person was adamant that they didn't want to be seen under their hood. However, Frank's guy took the liberty of sending us a magnified picture so that we could see. And sure enough, I knew that it was Ryan. My mouth was dry, my eyes searched the room for something to focus on, but before I knew it, everything went black. I opened my eyes and saw Frank leaning back in my armchair with a worried look on his face. I stretched my shoulders, neck and arms and rubbed my eyes clean.

"Did I pass out?"

"Yes. I was really worried about you. How are you feeling? Do you need to go to the hospital?"

I didn't need a hospital, no. What I needed were answers. It was getting late, and as much as I liked having Frank around to keep me company, I was beginning to wish that I was alone to process my emotions and thoughts. I was terrified that Ryan was after me, but the trepidation I felt was also wrapped in subconscious excitement. My skin tingled with the image of us making love in his apartment, and my heart thumped as I remembered the feeling of his lips tracing my neck.

"Are you listening?" Frank called me back to the room.

"I'm sorry, yes, I am."

"We need to set a trap so that you get to him before he gets to you and cause damage."

I was already damaged, but one thing I've learned in my life is that I had no time to sit and wallow in self-pity. I had to take care of myself and keep moving forward. Being in the position I was in; I knew I had leverage. Ryan didn't know how much resources I had, and even though I responded to his message, I doubt he was fully aware of the extent I was willing to go to put an end to this. He probably thought I was just an emotional broken little girl (with a lucky first kill) just like the rest of the men I've met.

"I'm fine, really, Frank. I'm ready to end this shit."

I walked to my bedroom and emerged with a small velvet bag. Inside, I had my special ready-made cocktail resting inside a syringe with a sterile needle.

"Izzy, you need to think this through. First, we need to set up a meeting to surprise him. Then you need to make sure you knock him out and do it quietly without being traced."

"I know that, Frank." My voice raised in agitation. "I fucked up the first time and brought this shit back to you. I can't put your life in danger anymore.

Frank relaxed his posture and hugged me. I felt reassured that I had the strength to finish this mess, once and for all.

"Right, I know it's getting late, but we need to start quickly. Let's go back to the hotel and surprise him."

We decided to have a drink in a quiet corner of the hotel bar to see if Ryan was inclined to a nightcap. We hung around for thirty minutes when I finally gave up and asked the bartender if he had seen him by producing a photo of Ryan on my phone. I flashed my most charismatic smile and bit my lip in persuasion. He relented and confirmed that the man in the picture is still a guest of the hotel who frequented the bar around lunchtime. I followed Frank's direction to his room and made my way to the 10th floor. As the lift ascended between each floor, I swallowed deep breaths to keep my heartbeat steady. Fortunately, only two people used the lift, which stopped two floors below my destination. When I reached the 10th floor, I took a deep breath and walked down the corridor to room 17. The summer heat was peaking, even at night, I had to settle on a simple dress and comfortable heels—chic, sexy and efficient. I knocked on the door and hid on the side so that he couldn't see me through the peephole. I waited for twenty seconds, and he didn't answer. Another knock and waited 20 more seconds and another, only this time the door abruptly opened. I was shocked to see his face remained as gorgeous as I remembered. And even with the look of surprise, a familiar beat of excitement lingered between us.

"Well, you look just as glorious as I remembered." I smirked as I walked into his room. "Quite basic for you. I should've known that you were slumming it. Sending me stupid messages with a poor vocabulary and expecting me to be intimidated."

He closed the door and stood there with darkness in his eyes. I wanted to run to him and tell him that I was sorry. Well, I wasn't sorry that I did what I did. I was sorry that it happened to him. But a lot had happened, it was too late for apologies. I was here to finish this once and for all.

"You have some balls on you bitch. Do you know how much you've fucked up my life?" He hissed.

"Correction, your brother and John fucked up your life. They also tried to fuck up mine, so I had to put an end to you all. Don't act so innocent because you were in on it too."

"Why the fuck are you here, Isabella?"

"Fancy a drink?" I raised my brow.

"If you think I'm going to drink or eat anything from you, you're out of your damn mind. I should kill you for coming here."

His words bounced on the floor as he spat and landed heavily on my chest. He looked like he'd been riding a rollercoaster to hell with his messy hair, dirty stubble, wearing jeans that should've been tossed in the bin. But his muscles were bigger even when the sparkle in his eyes had disappeared. If he wanted to, he could have dragged me across the floor and pound his fists into me, but I knew that's not the type of person he was. From the moment we met, I felt his energy was pure. Sure, we all have our burdens, but I knew that mine was somehow more significant. He was indeed a broken man thirsty for revenge. A slight vibration brought my attention to my watch, that was linked to receiving messages from my phone.

Hurry up.

It was from Frank. I had to stay focused and complete the job I went there to do.

"I know you're not stupid, Ryan. Look, I wanted to move on with my life, and you decided to summon me with your bullshit message. Clearly, I can't be rattled, and we deserve to have a conversation. I didn't come here to hurt you. Let's go down to the bar, have a drink and take it from there. If you want answers, I can give them to you, but you're not going lurk in the shadow to try and shake me down."

He agreed, and we made our descent to the hotel bar. Frank was still sitting tight at the table in the corner, that only I could notice. We planted ourselves on a table in the middle of the room closest to the bar. The bartender I spoke with earlier had left. Ryan ordered a beer, and I ordered a martini.

"Thought you only liked bourbon?"

"I like it all." I smirked.

"Why did you do it?" He stared straight into my eyes. Our drinks arrived, and I took a long sip.

Careful with the alcohol. Keep your head right.

Frank was growing impatient.

"You knew too much." I stared back at him.

"I was trying to help you, bitch!"

"Come on, Ryan. You were trying to help yourself because you were also involved in this mess. If you wanted to help me, you should've told me about your brother and that piece of shit John in the first place. Instead, you let me find out on my own after being entangled in this web. You were probably going to turn me in out of revenge for Andrew." I spat back.
All the talking was eating up my time, and I needed to get things moving back to the room I booked to end him. The room was booked under a pseudonym and paid for in cash. I finished my drink and excused myself for the bathroom. Frank promptly made his exit as he saw me walk towards the foyer.

"What the fuck is taking you so long?"

"He's very cautious, Frank, and we need to be careful. I don't think it's going to happen this soon. Go home, and I will call you when I leave. Trust me." He warily relented and got himself a taxi home. When I returned from the bathroom, I was surprised Ryan was still sitting there.

"You're still here."

"We're not done here. I'm warning you, Isabella, you will pay for what you've done."

"How come you're still alive, Ryan?" It was a question that weighed on my mind from the first time I saw his face on the photo.

"Rule number one. Always check that your victim is dead before you leave the scene."

I lost myself back then and slipped.

"Whatever it was you put in my drink, you mixed enough to cause some short-term damage but not enough to kill me. Amateur." He mocked. "John is dead in case you're wondering. But you need to remember that you're not the only one associated with criminals. Some of us are just better at hiding it".

I was tempted to do it right there as he sat with his inflated ego. But I did note that his next dose would be a lot larger than the first. I cleared my throat and pretended to feel guilty.

"I'm sorry." I broke down in tears, and for a second, I thought I saw his hard-exterior collapse. "I'm so sorry, Ryan. I didn't want to do it, but it all just closed in on me too quickly, and I panicked. I haven't been able to sleep in months."

"Wipe your eyes, Isabella. I didn't know you well back then, but after having some time to think I certainly know you now. My friends took my blood tests, and the ingredients you had in that cocktail were rare. Only a seasoned criminal or a severe drug addict would know how to get possession of them. You're not a severe drug addict as far as I can see. But right now, you are a criminal." He was right.

We were growing more agitated as customers diminished from the bar. It was approaching midnight, so I finished my second drink and announced that it was time for me to leave.

"Not so fast. You take one step outside; I'll have my guys take you on a trip that will make you wish you'd never messed with me." I wanted to test his threat. However, I needed to know what he knew. It didn't matter at this point, but his deep voice soothed me.

We made our way back to his room where my eyes traced everything in sight, looking for anything he could have concealed to hurt me. I sat on the awkward armchair next to the bed prompting him to continue the conversation. It happened so fast that I didn't have time to savour the moment. All I felt was my skin tingling as his hands rubbed my thighs while his lips bit and slid around my neck. The broken look on his face was no longer present as he kissed every inch of my body.

Heat engulfed between my thighs as my hands rubbed every inch of his muscles, pulling him closer to me as though I was scared that he would evaporate and vanish in a dream. No, it wasn't a dream. Something changed in the situation between the martinis and the journey to his room. Even though he was still seeking revenge and thoughts of murder swirled in both of our minds, I knew that he also felt a strong connection between us. We kissed for what felt like an eternity before he pressed himself into me with his hands clasped into mine. His arms flexed as he balanced his body on top of me. His eyes were glazed with lust, and his desire beckoned me to accept him, to pull him closer and prompt him to thrust harder and faster. The air was thick with words that were not exchanged between us. My nails dug deep into his back as he thrust himself inside me. The feeling of his skin rubbing onto mine as sweat slid down our bodies was pure ecstasy. A euphoric feeling emerged as an incredible orgasm tore through me.

"Fuck." He groaned as he came with me.

We collapsed in silence for a short time as I wondered whether I should be the one to speak first.

"You're still a great fuck." He said as he walked to the bathroom. An attempt to divert the intensity of the act we just committed together. My phone quickly buzzed me back to reality.

Is it done? I'm getting worried. CALL ME.

Frank was sitting on the edge of his seat and rightfully so since I would have to tell him about the diversion of our plan. I quickly got dressed and fixed my hair as I heard Ryan in the shower. I rummaged around the room and found his wallet on the floor. I shoved it into my bag, double-checking that the cocktail of death was still in its velvet package. There was no chance that he saw it because the case was locked. Grabbing my bag and shoes, I left before he even had the chance to finish his shower. I took a cab to Frank's apartment, which was not far from the hotel.

"What the fuck have you been doing?" Frank demanded as he greeted me in his corridor.

"I messed up Frank." I carefully said avoiding the chance to give him a heart attack. "I slept with him." I bit my lip.

"You went there to kill him, and you end up fucking him? Are you crazy?" He walked to the kitchen and took a shot of tequila.

"I know. I mean, I don't know how it happened, one minute we were bickering at the bar and the next we were in his bed. If it's any consolation, it was just animal instincts, and it didn't mean anything." I lied.

"Izzy, it's nearly 2 a.m., and you didn't call or text to let me know you're okay. Your reckless behaviour is dangerous, and it puts both of us in danger."

"I'm sorry, Frank. We will find a way to sort this. I promise. I took his wallet." I smiled.

"Oh my god. He's going to be pissed when he notices that it's gone. Then he'll come here looking for you since he hand-delivered that note. Shit."

We continued our conversation until dawn when we eventually fell asleep in Frank's bed. I awoke at 10 a.m., showered and borrowed Frank's shirt fashioned into a dress to avoid doing the walk of shame back to my apartment. Frank and I decided that it would be better if we waited for Ryan to initiate contact with me, which would give us an edge over the situation. As the cab driver weaved around traffic, I wondered whether killing Ryan would put a stop this mess. Or perhaps deep down I knew that I didn't want to lose him because I was in love with him. Although I slept soundly in Frank's bed, as soon as I entered my home, my safe place, I collapsed into a ball on the sofa and cried. I cried for the life that I wished I manifested instead of the mess I was in. I cried for Ryan. I cried for Frank, and his unrelenting support which dragged him deeper into danger and I cried for my parents. I hadn't thought about them for a long time. In a state of internal crisis, I missed them, and I needed them.

Chapter Six

Frank

I knew that something was off with Izzy when I left her at the hotel. She usually had no problems doing what needed to be done in any situation, but somehow, Ryan had managed to get under her skin and made her lose focus. I dreaded going home because since Mathew left, it had not been the same. The smell of his cooking would usually greet me as I walked through the front door, and when he was in an excellent mood, the melody of his humming echoed around the apartment. Now, the rooms were empty, like my heart. I messaged and called Mathew a few times to no avail, so I decided to leave the situation as it was. If we were meant to be together, then he would find his way back to me. It was now Saturday; however, it felt like Isabella and I had been paddling through this Ryan crisis for months rather than a few days. When she left my apartment around 10.a.m. I decided to stay in bed for a few more hours to catch up on sleep although, the summer heat was at its peak, so I decided to have a shower, get dressed and bring some lunch to Isabella. It was nice that we were spending a lot of time together, even if it was under the unfortunate circumstance. My independence in relationships, friendships and finance was of great importance but, since Isabella and I reconnected, I found myself gravitating further towards her. We were both different and growing into our strengths yet, we still enjoyed our bourbons and the occasional high. The afternoon heat sizzled on my neck as I stood on the pavement and waved my hand for a cab to Isabella's apartment.

"I brought lunch," I said as she opened the door when I noticed her brown eyes were puffy and bare. "What's wrong?"

She ran into my arms, and I held her tight. "I don't think I can do this anymore, Frank." She sobbed.

We stood in the middle of her living room for a moment. I understood that she needed a good cry so that she could move forward with clarity. And all I had to do was let her cry out her frustration and hurt until she had the strength to pull herself back together.

"You know that whatever you decide to do, I'll support you." We were now sat on her sofa picking at our lunchtime salads.

"I know, and I'm grateful. I'm just so confused, Frank. Ryan and I both felt something, in an ideal world, we would call it a day, you know, no harm done. Kiss and makeup."

"Don't be ridiculous darling. We don't live in an ideal world. It's eat or be eaten in our world. Has he messaged you about his wallet?"

"Yes. He's pissed. I've gone through it." She pulled the wallet out from under the coffee table and handed it to me.

The wallet had a few credit cards under different names, fake ID cards and one thousand pounds in cash.

"We've been running around the city collecting dirt on Andrew and John, but we never stopped to wonder what sort of shit Ryan was involved in," I said as I analysed the credit cards. "Do you know how difficult it is to get an AMEX these days? He must know some naughty people to get one on a fake name. Did you ever wonder how the hell he lived and left the hotel without a trace?"

"He said the dose I gave him caused short term damage. I didn't check he was dead before I left. Fuck. He also said that his friends did a blood test to see what was given to him. It's worth considering that he's probably just like us except he's good at tucking his tail between his legs." She spat.

"Yeah, I know if I were in the same position my guys would help me out. It still doesn't explain the lack of information about the case online."

"A lot didn't make sense with Andrew, but he still fucked up our lives anyway."

We pondered in silence for a moment.

"So, what now?"

"I'll arrange to meet and give Ryan back his wallet. In exchange for some information."

Isabella sent a message to Ryan, arranging to meet him at the bar across the road from his hotel. She was confident that he would show up because he needed his wallet. It was approaching 4 p.m. when she received a reply to meet Ryan immediately. I shook my head at the audacity of him, summoning her at his convenience. We agreed for Isabella to meet him alone so that he continues to think I did what he asked in the note and kept away from the situation. I wasn't comfortable letting Isabella meeting him on her own considering what happened the last time she did, so I chose to wait for her in a deli across the road from the hotel which was not too far from the bar. Ryan commanded a meeting at 5 p.m., which gave us enough time to eat something light and set up a recording device in Isabella's bag.

"Whatever you do, don't leave your bag unattended."

"I won't. We'll see what he says then work out our next step from there."

We both grabbed our necessities and made our way out the door. As we walked out of the main entrance, my heart lunged itself at the walls of my chest. My head was spinning as I tried to steady my breath. Mathew crossed the road with a man that was about my height and build. Isabella linked her arm in mine, attempting to anchor my emotions.

"Hi there," I said through gritted teeth. The audacity of this man to move on so quickly.

"Frank, hi. How have you been?" He asked, and I made a point to introduce myself to his new friend.

"I've been great Mathew. And yourself?" I smiled.

"Amazing. Well, it was nice to bump into you. Take care." Isabella watched as they continued their journey down the road.

"That man is anything but amazing." Isabella mocked. I gave a slight nod, and we hailed a cab to Aldwych.

Even though I looked great, my mood wasn't quite as good after seeing Mathew. I would've been lying if I said it didn't hurt me to see him moved on with someone else. The cab dropped Isabella at the bar to meet Ryan, and I decided to get a massage from a therapist not too far from them instead of waiting inside a greasy deli. The recording device I set up in Isabella's handbag was synced to my phone, which enabled me to listen remotely. The masseuse wasn't excited that I had my headphones on during the massage, but I didn't care. It prevented her awkward small talk.

Isabella

We sat for ten excruciating minutes before Ryan said his first word. I made sure to wear the most fashionable outfit I owned, opting to look well put together but not over the top.

"My wallet." He prompted.

"I had a look inside, the credit cards are not in your name, and neither are the identity cards. It seems that you are involved with some naughty people Ryan." I pursed my lips, as I looked directly at him.

"Well, because of you, I couldn't go back to work for a while and was dismissed. How else was I going to make money?"

"Understandable, but you still have to build a rapport with those kinds of people. You don't just order fake credit cards like you're ordering a takeaway meal. In this case, I'm not the only criminal, after all." I playfully said.

We danced in silence for a moment, and I kept my awareness on him even when I looked at the other patrons around the bar.

"So, here's what you're going to do. You're going to pack up everything you have and leave this country for good."

"I don't think so." I spat back.

"Oh, yes, you are. Because I've had about enough of your shit. Either you leave, or I report everything to the police and send you to prison. As much as I like your edge, I don't think that a beautiful woman like you would survive there."

He was right. I had an edge, but I wouldn't survive in prison. However, I was sure that I was not going to leave the country. I smiled to myself after noticing that he said he liked my edge. Ryan was sitting back in his chair with a smug look on his face, although the darkness in his eyes was still there. I nodded and grabbed my bag to head for the door. He followed behind, and as we stood on the pavement, wondering which way to go, he pulled me into him and kissed me hard. I was taken by surprise although, I relaxed my shoulders and leaned into him. His lips were soft, and his face was now stubble-free. Our mouths stayed glued on each other's for a while as we savoured what he thought was the last kiss. He then broke our embrace and walked towards the hotel.

Where are you? I'm leaving.

I messaged Frank.

We met inside a quaint Italian restaurant not far from the hotel. Frank bought two bourbons as it was very much needed since I knew that he was listening to the conversation.

"I can't believe he kissed you."

"Clearly, he still wants me. I've come a long way, Frank, I am not leaving the country, and I can't go to prison."

"He's bluffing Izzy. He doesn't have any proof. He doesn't know where Andrew's body was disposed of. There's no footage of what happened in Cumbria. Otherwise, he would've gone turned you in ages ago. He's hurt, but he needs to get over it and move on. Besides, we have proof of him blackmailing you and admitting to possessing fake credit cards."

"I know Frank, but I've done things in my past that will raise enough suspicion with the police if he keeps digging and actually turns me in." I took a long sip of my drink while Frank waited for an answer.

I had never told anyone about what happened to my mother or Paul back in Dorset. Nor did I want to raise the memory of it now, but Frank had stood by me since this all started, and I owed him the truth. I just hoped that he stayed after he heard it.

"When I was seventeen, my mum died. Her boyfriend killed her." Frank's mouth dropped open as my eyes began to glaze with moisture.

"My dad died first, and we descended into debt. Shortly after, my mum started drinking loads and met Paul, who was physically abusive. One night I snapped when I heard him hitting her. I blacked out and hit him on the head with a baseball bat. I did everything to cover my back, and when the police came, they assumed I was innocent because I was a minor, and I explained that Paul killed my mum. I then moved to a foster family in Salisbury until I turned eighteen and decided to move to London. I had never looked back since."

Frank drained his bourbon and asked the waiter for another as soon as my mouth stopped moving. He moved closer to me and held my hand.

"Thank you for telling me this, and I promise that it stays with me. We all have demons and baggage, but nothing's changed between us. We'll be careful."

My lungs deflated as I exhaled a breath of relief. We were too far down the criminal road for me to lose him, and even though I had never told him, my heart loved everything about him. We ordered some food and bounced ideas of how we were going to approach the Ryan situation. We knew that he would never leave us in peace unless he was offered something difficult for him to say no to, perhaps if we offered him a new life.

"Frank, I have assets that I can liquidate and give to Ryan. He said I fucked up his life and he didn't seem to care much about Andrew. Maybe if I offered him enough cash, he could just disappear." I bit my lip.

"Okay. Cash is good, but he's not cheap, Izzy."

"Don't worry about what I can afford. I know people and most of my clients have helped me invest along the way."

Frank smirked at my revelation. We finished dinner, and I decided it was time for me to visit Ryan at his hotel, leaving Frank to his own devices for the rest of the evening. He was a grown man, after all, and he needed to have some fun.

I stood outside room 17 and stared at the door. My heart was racing, and my mind raced with a thousand thoughts. I wanted to turn and run the other way. Just as I decided to leave, the door opened.

"What the fuck?" He said as he emerged from the room wearing a fitted t-shirt and shorts. I swallowed the lump in my throat and glared at him for a moment.

"Look, I'm not leaving."

"Yes, you are."

"No, I am not!" I firmly said. "I know you're hurt and don't pretend that what we had back then wasn't real because it was. It seems that all you want is your old life back. I can't go back in time Ryan, but I can help you build a new one. You can't live like this forever." I walked into his room, and he promptly closed the door. His breath was rising, and the veins on his neck grew with his anger.

"I can give you the money you need to start over."

"I don't want your money." He said through gritted teeth.

"No, you just want money on your fake credit cards which I'm sure has a shelf life. Take my offer, Ryan. Fifty Thousand Pounds cash is yours to disappear, for good. A clean slate, away from me." I stared at him as he clenched his jaw and thought about the offer.

"It's not going to this easy for you Isabella."

"Fine. Then I'll make it easy for the police when I claim that you are blackmailing me and admitted having possession on fake credit cards. This will then start an investigation with your old employers, your credit card plug, and anyone who's helped you acquire them. And those people will most likely have their lives and reputation ruined too." I played him the recording from my phone and reminded him that I had copies.

"You are unbelievable."

"Take the money, Ryan. You can do anything and go anywhere you want and start fresh." All in a sudden, tears cascaded down my cheeks. At that moment, I realised that I was conflicted. I wanted him, the problem was gone, but I was also saddened by the idea that I would never see him again. We stood and looked at each other for a moment, and I swore I saw his eyes soften. I wanted to leap into his arms and hold him for eternity. Instead, I walked to his bathroom and found some tissue to wipe my eyes and splashed some water on my face. I felt pathetic and embarrassed that he saw me like this. I looked at myself in the mirror and smiled at the gorgeous reflection that looked back. I knew that regardless of what happened, I was not going to give up without a fight. Suddenly, Ryan walked in and softly kissed my cheek.

"My mind wants to kill you. But my heart wants to kiss your soft lips." His face was so close to mine that his cologne lingered and appeased my nostrils. My heart rate increased, and I could feel his breath on me. He leaned in closer and lightly bit my bottom lip. I pulled his mouth into mine, and we kissed for a while. I lifted his t-shirt, exposing his taut stomach and bulky arms. He lifted my skirt as I wrapped my legs around his waist and slowly slid inside me, sending electricity up my spine that erupted into euphoria. I closed my eyes in pleasure, but he cupped my neck and placed his thumb on my cheek, prompting me to look at him.

"Look into me, Isabella." We held our gaze as he worked himself in and out of me. We lost ourselves in the moment, and I took a mental picture of us, frozen in time.

We halted as our heart raced in ecstasy. He gently lowered my legs to the floor and walked to the bedroom. I leaned against the wall for a minute then freshened up as I came to terms to reality.

"Okay. Fifty thousand in a week and I'll be gone." He said with coldness as I walked into the room. I nodded in agreement, grabbed my bag and left. Nothing else was said, and nothing needed to be said. The situation was too complicated to linger on feelings. As I walked down the corridor to the lift, I messaged Frank for his location.

Club Rouge.

I exited the hotel and hailed a cab to *Club Rouge*. When I walked in, I met Frank and his colleagues at the bar. We had a few memories of that club, and I guessed Frank was there in hopes of bumping into Mathew since it's where they first met. Club *Rouge* was also the place to be on a hot Saturday night.

"Hello, gorgeous." Frank greeted and introduced me to his colleagues. I shook each of their hands, and my eyes especially lingered on his handsome manager, Colin.

We ordered a few rounds of drinks, and I told Frank about the circumstance of a few hours earlier with Ryan. I didn't need to elaborate on how I felt as Frank could see it mirrored in my eyes. The evening progressed into ecstasy as Frank, and I danced until my legs started to ache and I talked to Colin in between breaks. He was a lovely man, and I was attracted to him. Colin was the type of man looking to settle down with his third wife, he was in his early forties and already made his fortune by investing well into the gallery. All I heard in the conversation was his potential to be one of my clients. Nonetheless, I worked my magic and soothed his ego by telling him how much of a gentleman he was, while confirming that all I needed was for a man to look after me. I checked my phone to see that it was 11 p.m. and told Frank that I was leaving with Colin in tow.

"Oh my god, I want to know everything tomorrow." He laughed. "I'm going home too. Might call Lars for a playdate."

We said our goodbyes and exited the club. The cab ride back to my apartment was full of conversation. Colin and I were buzzed but not drunk enough to act stupid and careless. I learned that he loved to read historical fiction and play golf in his downtime. But ultimately, curating contemporary art was his love. Colin was impressed with my home décor when we walked into my apartment.

"Would you like a drink? I have wine and organic tequila" I smiled.

"Tequila sounds good." He said as he admired my wall pieces.

We reclined on the sofa and chatted for a while before Colin leaned in kissed me.

"Look, I don't sleep with men I meet in clubs for free. I-"

"You love money and want to know my net worth before you give up the goods." He smirked. I was impressed that I didn't have to strategize the game. Colin, like most of my clients, was well established and familiar with the game. If he wasn't going to spend money on me, whether he guessed I was an escort or not, wealthy men knew that high-class women always had a price. So, he reached for his wallet and placed two thousand pounds on the table and smiled.

"Do something fabulous for yourself in the morning. A spa perhaps?" My inside cringed when I heard the word spa as I placed the memory of Ryan and John in the far corner of my mind.

"Now, where were we?" I smiled.

We made love on the sofa. Colin was no Ryan or Andrew, but like many of my clients, he was pleasant. Gentle and determined to make me feel safe and desired. He left my apartment an hour later.

Chapter Seven

Frank

I couldn't help but call Mathew when I left *Club Rouge*. It would've been easier to call Lars over to spend the night, but my heart didn't want that.

"It's Frank. I want to see you and talk." I cringed at the words that came out of my mouth into Mathew's voicemail.

I had a long hot shower when I arrived home and hit the vape to calm my mind. My bed invited me to lounge into a blissful state. The doorbell rang just as my eyelids slammed shut. My heart started to race as I made my way to the door. Mathew stood and smiled.

"Aren't you going to invite me in?" I beckoned him inside.

"You should still use your key. I know we're not together anymore, but you still have some of your clothes here." Just as I finished, Mathew kissed me and wrapped his arms around me. I leaned into him, and tears started to run down my face because I knew deep in my heart that I loved him, and I wanted him to stay.

We kissed for several minutes and made our way to the bedroom. I was about to take his t-shirt off, but he stopped.

"I'm not here for this Frank. We need to talk, well I need to talk." I sat on the bed and listened.

"We were so good together, and you hurt me, Frank. You have to understand that I made a commitment to you which you threw out without regards."

"I know. I thought I didn't care enough to be sorry for what I did, but I am sorry because I regret hurting you and I miss you. When you met me, I was a selfish boy who hated responsibility, but then you helped me to grow. There's no excuse for what I did Mathew, but I will say that I was growing so much love for having a home with you that it scared me."

"What were you scared of?"

"I feared losing myself. I feared not having the space to do what I normally did when I was single."

"Frank, I never expressed concerned, which prevented you from doing what you wanted. I know how close you and Isabella are and would never dream of breaking you two apart."

We sat in silence for a moment as I decided it was time for me to tell him about my secret troubles.
"I know, but there's a lot about me you don't know." I paused for a breath. "You have to understand that what I'm about to tell you has nothing to do with you and you will not be dragged into it."

"Sounds worrying. What's going on, Frank?"

"The night I met you at *Club Rouge*, Isabella and I were being blackmailed by someone. He was closing in so fast that it felt like a noose around my neck. The whole situation was so messy, and we were playing a game of chess with the devil. Long story short, the person disappeared, and we thought it was going to be okay, but their friend is back. He has some dirt on Isabella, so we're trying to get him to leave."

"Why not go to the police?"

"That's out of the question." He kept pushing for answers that I had but didn't want to tell him. I wanted to tell Mathew the truth. However, I had to do whatever it took to protect Isabella.

"You're involved in some deep shit, and that's fine if you don't want to tell me, but if we're going to start over, there can't be any secrets between us."

"You want to start over, for real?" It was a pleasant surprise to hear him say those words. "Fine. Isabella is an escort."

"So?" He stared blankly. "A lot of women are escorts in this city."

"Yes, and she also took advantage of someone, which is why they blackmailed her. And I was collateral damage. Anyway, the situation is complicated, but I assure you, I'm keeping it away from us."

I didn't have to explain further as Mathew knew when it was time to drop the subject. As much as I wanted to tell him, I was afraid that dragging him into the situation would put him in danger. For now, it was better for me to reassure him and focus on mending our relationship. We didn't sleep together that night which was comforting. We snuggled in each other's arms until the next morning.

"Hey. I have to get ready for work." He yawned.

"It's Sunday." I pouted.

"I know, but I have rent to pay."

"Move back in with me. It'll be cheaper, and things will be different this time."

"I trust that it will but in time. For now, we need to take one step at a time." He kissed me and made his way to the door. "I'll call you when I'm done, and we can have dinner."

Just like that, we had kissed and made up. It was all the reassurance I needed to know that everything was going to work out fine.

Isabella decided to cook Sunday lunch at her apartment, which gave us time to decide how she was going to pull the money together for Ryan.

"I have just over twenty-five thousand in cash, and the rest is on the market." She chirped as she chopped and sautéed the vegetables. "I contacted one of my clients for a favour. He's going to sell and help me withdraw on Monday."

"You're practically superwoman." I teased, and we both giggled.

She looked effortlessly beautiful and at ease while cooking. I poured us a glass of Barolo each and sipped.

"Mathew and I made up, but I had to tell him about your profession and that we are in a bit of a situation. That's all he knows because let's face it, the less he knows, the better for his safety. Anyway, he wasn't surprised when I told him about your job."

"I'm glad you two made up, but there are things that he definitely shouldn't know." She raised her brows.

"I'm not stupid. Love is great but dangerous when it turns sour. Besides, I helped get rid of Andrew. I'm just as involved."

We drained our glass of wine, and I poured another. Sunday lunch was delicious, and I enjoyed the ceremonious ritual of helping Isabella set the table and create a cosy atmosphere. White and red scented candles were also lit around the living room. We enjoyed a beautifully roasted lamb with potatoes and veg. The afternoon progressed peacefully as the wine buzzed through our system. I helped Izzy clean up and box the leftovers for my evening snack before I made my way home.

Isabella

It was great to have Sunday lunch with Frank which helped take my mind off things. As I worked my way around the kitchen preparing the meal, I felt all my problems disappear for a moment. After Frank left, I called one of my clients to collect a favour he owed me. He had suspicions that his wife was stealing money from him before their divorce and asked me to follow and watch her report my findings. At the time, such a job was out of my remit although, I did it as a favour since he always paid me well. He didn't hesitate to sell my stocks and confirmed the money would be in my account within twenty-four hours. Monday arrived when I awoke to a heavy knock on the door. My hair was messy, and my skin was dehydrated. However, I was more concerned with the loud thuds coming from the corridor.

"Colin, it's 9 a.m. What are you doing here?" What I wanted to ask was how did he remember the direction to my apartment, but I let it slide.

"The other night was phenomenal. I want to do it again." I looked at him for a moment, wondering if he thought the other night was a one-off or knew that I was a professional who was in the game for the long run.

"I'm sorry for assuming. I don't care if this is your thing or not." He confirmed as though he read my mind. "Five thousand pounds for a night." He continued.

I decided it was time to let him come in so that we could discuss business. We sat at the dining table as I revealed that I was a high paid escort who only dated affluent men. My price was negotiable; however, five thousand pounds would not suffice. My days of being cheap were long gone. Colin didn't seem surprised by my revelation, and I wasn't offended. I was a professional, and my goal was to make money. We decided to meet for dinner on Wednesday evening at Hotel Aldwych. I thought it would be a perfect way to see if Ryan was still lurking around and yes perhaps, I also wanted to make him jealous. Frank wasn't too happy with this arrangement considering Colin was his boss, but I promised that if Colin didn't give me a reason to start trouble, then it wouldn't be an issue. Besides, since the Andrew situation occurred, I had no choice but to be extra careful with clients which meant that they had to sign a non-disclosure agreement and always pay the money upfront. The transaction, of course, was non-refundable if the date was cancelled for any reason.

Wednesday evening arrived, and I made sure I looked my best for my date with Colin. I poured myself in a custom-made red pencil dress paired with a pair of pointed pumps. My hair was straight with new highlights, and my eyes were lined with false eyelashes for the drama. Colin offered to pick me up, but I insisted it was best practice that I booked a cab there myself. This always allowed me to make an entrance. The cab dropped me outside the hotel where I made my entrance meet with the concierge and confirm that I was here for dinner with Colin at the restaurant. The host walked me to the restaurant where I saw Colin had booked a booth and elegantly decorated it with a few stems of roses. Colin immediately stood up when he saw me and admired my attire.

"Isabella you look gorgeous as always I'm glad we finally agreed. Is everything okay on your end?" I nodded with content know that my money was safely tucked away in my bank account.

Dinner conversation picked up between the starter and main course. I kept to a three drinks maximum rule to keep a clear head. Colin unsurprisingly couldn't keep his eyes off me. Just as the desserts arrived, the hairs on the back on my neck stood to attention as I saw Ryan approach the bar. I excused myself and walked towards the toilet. His face froze when he saw me, but I glanced over him like any other patrons of the restaurant. He lightly touched my arm as I reached the foyer.

"What the fuck do you think you're doing?"

"I'm on a date." I smiled and attempted to walk away.

"You've got some nerve to come here and-

"And what? You don't own this hotel, Ryan. You've accepted the offer. Your money is on the way. We are done here." I quickly walked to the bathroom, as my heart started racing.

When I walked back to the restaurant, Ryan was still perched at the bar with a bourbon in his hand. I walked directly past him to continue my date with Colin.

"Are you okay?"

"Yes, I'm fine." I smiled.

Dessert was delicious, but I couldn't enjoy it properly as I could feel Ryan's eyes on me. Colin had booked a room in the hotel, so we decided to move our date upstairs. The lift took us to the penthouse suite that had a jaw-dropping view of the city. The summer sun was setting that painted a romantic backdrop for our date. The evening ended pleasantly. Colin and I both got what we wanted. I didn't usually sleepover with my clients, and when I announced it was time for me to leave, Colin gave me some cash for a cab. I arrived home at 11 p.m.

I contemplated calling Frank for a night out; however, my feet were aching, and I assumed he was mending his relationship with Mathew, and I was not going to interrupt their time together. I kicked off my shoes, hung up my dress for dry cleaning and submerged myself in a hot bubble bath. My mind drifted in a meditative trance, and I saw nothing but comforting blackness. I was in the bath for twenty minutes when I heart a subtle knock on the door. I assumed it was Frank, so I jumped out of the bath and wrapped myself in a silk robe as I walked to answer.

"Ryan." I was stunned and anxious. "How did you know where I lived?"

"I followed you. Isn't that what you wanted Isabella.?" He walked past me and admired my apartment.

"What are you doing here? We had an arrangement. Perhaps it has something to do with the other night?" I slowly walked towards him and dropped my robe.

"I'm not here for that." He said as I walked to the kitchen and poured us both a glass of wine, making a point to open a new bottle to ease his trust.

"Well, you're obviously here for something." I smirked as I sipped some wine and handed him the same glass.

We danced around the chase until Ryan relented. He moved closer and grabbed my waist.

"I hated seeing you with another man. Is that the type of men you like?" There was no way I was confirming Colin was a client. It was safer to let him assume it was an expected date. Besides, it was more fun to see jealousy in his eyes.

"Maybe, sounds like you're jealous." He pulled me in harder and traced his lips on my neck.

He moved his mouth down my neck towards my shoulders and my breasts as his hand stayed firmly around my waist. There was enough heat between us to spark a flame and light the building on fire. I let my body linger in his embrace and enjoyed his warmth. His arm muscles were flexed as I jumped and wrapped my legs around his waist. He carried me to the bedroom, threw me on the bed and climbed on top of me, halted for a moment to look into my eyes. I could tell his mind swirled with thoughts he didn't know how to express with words. He took a deep breath and rolled off me laying on his back, and the only thing that could be heard between us was the beat of our hearts.

"I'm not here for that." He exhaled. Surprised, I rolled onto my side and traced my hand on his arm.

"Then, why are you here?" I waited patiently for an answer.

"I'm here because I can't bear to see you with another man."

We laid on the bed for a while, as I tried to resist the smirk that was growing on my face. This was the first time that Ryan and I laid in bed together without kissing or having sex. Minutes passed and eventually, hours before he stood up and walked to the bathroom. My heart was on edge as I didn't know what to expect. One minute he wanted to kill me, and the next minute he was in my bed telling me that he did not want to see me with another man. Part of me wanted to tell him that the date wasn't, in fact, a real date and that I was getting paid for it, however, I was still cautious as his moves and actions were unpredictable. Ryan returned from the bathroom and climbed back into bed.

"I thought you were getting ready to leave?"

"Nope. I'm spending the night with you. Is that a problem?"

It wasn't a problem, but I didn't particularly appreciate playing the guessing game. Nonetheless, it felt nice to sleep next to him and absorb his warmth. Morning arrived, and I rolled over to find an empty space next to me. My heart started to race as I climbed out of bed to check the safe was still locked. I exited the bedroom, and I could smell the coffee fumes lingering from the kitchen.

"Good morning, I see that you're an early riser just like me." And there he was, in my kitchen cooking breakfast.

"What's on the menu this morning chef?" I walked to the kitchen and sat at the island.

"Well, I wasn't sure if you ate meat, was a vegetarian or a vegan considering that everyone has a dietary requirement these days so, I decided it was safer to go vegan. Vegan pancakes with blueberries."

We sat and had breakfast like a normal couple, and for a moment, it felt nice. I felt like nothing had happened in the last year and a half of my life. Then it hit me, that after this moment I would deliver the money to Ryan, he would leave, and I would never see him again. I think that on some level, Ryan was doing this to ease the pain of separation between us, perhaps it was his last attempt to create something real and concrete before he disappeared forever. By Thursday evening, I received a call from my client to confirm that the transaction had been completed and the twenty-five thousand pounds should now be available in my bank account. So, I decided to call Ryan to confirm how he wanted his money delivered. It turned out that he had legitimate bank accounts to hold the twenty-five thousand pounds and he confirmed that he wanted the rest in cash and lucky for me, the money was already sitting in a bag inside my safe. I called Frank to confirm that everything was sorted with the money and that I was going to deliver the cash in person on Saturday morning.

Chapter Eight

Frank

I couldn't believe my ears when Izzy told me that Ryan slept over at her apartment. I was even more stunned when she confirmed that they spent the whole night together but didn't have sex. My heart broke when she revealed that she would drop the money to Ryan on Saturday morning, which would prompt him to leave as early as Saturday evening if he already had a plan. I decided it was time to find out if this was what Ryan wanted. Mathew had received a new temporary job contract in Kent, so he was gone for two weeks which gave me enough time to concentrate my attention on Isabella and Ryan. I took a cab to Hotel Aldwych and marched to Ryan's room on the 10th floor.

"Hi." I modestly said when he opened the door. I anticipated that he wouldn't have been happy to see me since I contributed to the fuckery of his life however, I trusted that Izzy hadn't divulged the level of my involvement of his brother and John's death.

"Do you want to leave the country?" I asked.

"It's none of your business what I want to do. And if you and Isabella weren't in my life in the first place, then I wouldn't be in this position."

"Look, you don't know much about me, but I know that you are aware that I would do anything to help Isabella in this situation. Before your brother and John decided to fuck around and blackmail us, believe it or not, Isabella and I didn't trust each other. All we had in common was the love for parties and party favours. What I do know for sure is that she has never cared about any man the way she has grown to care about you. Things are complicated between you, but everything's done now, and you can both choose to move forward together." I walked to the minibar, took two beers and handed one to Ryan.

"You know when I found out about Andrew. All I felt was a relief." I stared at him blankly. It seemed that we all had secrets and burdens in this situation.

"I felt relieved because I knew that he was the devil reincarnated. Since we were kids, Andrew always got himself into trouble, and I had to bail him out. When our parents died, he spiralled out of control. Partied with random strangers and got into fights and eventually, he messed around with women. I'm sure Isabella told you about Juliana. At first, I thought she could help Andrew turn his life around. She was sweet and patient with him. She had her life together. But then, he got possessive and abusive. I told her she had to commit to herself, and I encouraged her to get a restraining order against him. I helped her with her story, and he eventually phased out of her life." He sipped his beer.

"Do you have feelings for Juliana?" It was a question I had to ask.

"No, she's just a friend."

"Do you still see her?"

"Nope. My life is a mess. She doesn't need to be in it." He took another sip. "I know I'm not a fugitive, but after missing work for a long time, they had to let me go, and I needed money, so I'm surviving on fake credit cards and identities."

"I'm sorry that all of this happened to you, I am, but you have to understand that everyone had a part to play in the situation. However, it's not too late for you to rebuild. You don't have to leave the country once you collect that money, Ryan. Just find somewhere to settle in the city and start over."

"No good can come from me staying here. Too much has happened, and even though I love Isabella, I also resent her." I perked up as I heard him confess his love for Izzy. It sounded so right, and I knew deep within my heart that they could have a future. Ryan and I managed to push past our differences, and we came to a mutual agreement that some questions were better left, not asked. I left and headed to the bar since it was still early Thursday evening.

Come by the apartment. Need some company.

I finished my drink and took a cab to see Izzy. We ordered sushi and ate it on her balcony as the sound of traffic swirled beneath us. People of all shapes and background walked along the pavement. Some made their way to restaurants and clubs, while others made their way home from their jobs.

"I went to see Ryan." She looked at me in shock.

"He's in love with you." We paused for a moment.

"He said that?" She pressed.

"He also said he resented you."

"I honestly don't know what to think or feel anymore, Frank. I missed the days when Everything was simple. There's nothing I can do to change his mind. It is what it is. I'll give him the money on Saturday, and we can both go our separate ways." She drained her wine glass.

Somehow, I wasn't convinced that she was content with going separate ways. She admitted that she was falling in love with Ryan, and I knew she was calm about it to save face when he left.

"Did he mention where he will go once you give him the money?"

"No. And I think that it would be best for all of us if I did it know." She poured herself another glass of wine.

"Yes, because otherwise you would be tempted to chase him down and profess your love for him darling." I teased.

We finished our sushi and continued to watch the world go by. Suddenly, I decided that we should go out dancing however, it was time we went somewhere other than *Club Rouge*. It was just after 11 p.m. so I suggested that we went back to *Bar Hugh* as Lars and I were cordial and had mutual respect one another. He encouraged me to work things out with Mathew, and I thought he was one person who earned some room in my circle.

"Won't Matthew be upset about us going back to where Lars is working?" Izzy giggled as she got ready in her room.

"Everything I did was on me. Lars was the one who encouraged me to work things out with Matthew, and if we're rebuilding trust, I don't see why there should be a problem. Lars is just a friend now. Besides, Matthew has left me alone for two weeks. We are likely to have some free drinks tonight, so I won't tell if you don't." We both giggled as I checked my phone to see that the cab had arrived.

Bar Hugh was busier than the last time we went there, so we made our way to the bar where Lars greeted us with a welcoming smile. Izzy opted for a mini dress that hugged her curves, yet she still managed to look sophisticated. Everyone was looking at her, and I felt proud to be with her. We asked the host for a booth however, she confirmed that they were all reserved.

"Very well, then. We'll just have to find a free table in a dark corner." I teased.

We eventually found a table on the far corner of the bar. It was close enough to carry the drinks over without risk of bumping into people but far enough not to be bothered by large lurking groups. Thirty minutes passed when Izzy pulled me in the middle to dance. As we glided and bumped our hips, a sudden bolt of electricity shot through my chest.

"What's wrong?" Suddenly, I couldn't breathe, and I was desperate to purge the lump out of my throat.

I approached the group with caution to confirm what I saw, and there was Mathew, kissing the handsome man he was walking with after we broke up. I stood there for what felt like an eternity, waiting for them to break their embrace and to see the look on his face when he saw me. Isabella stood right next to me and held my hand tight, trying to pull me away from the situation, but my body wouldn't move. Pain radiated in my chest as I clenched the muscles in my jaw. Mathew eventually saw me, but it was too late. I leapt towards them and punched his friend in the face. People rushed to separate us, and I could hear Isabella shouting, but I continued pounding my fists into him. The bouncers eventually pulled me away and escorted us outside. My fists were bruised, but I smiled, knowing that the guy's face was no longer handsome.

"What the hell happened in there?" Lars came over to us outside.

"Mathew said he was working in Kent for two weeks and I saw him in there kissing some guy. Sorry, I fucked up."

Lars said it was best that we didn't come back to the bar for a while, and I agreed. Isabella and I took a cab back to my place. Mathew called and left voicemails, but I refused to deal with him. What I did to him was a momentary lapse whereas, he went out of his way to lie to me about working so that he could get it on with someone else in a bar. The adrenaline from the wine and fighting had subsided, I needed cloudiness to calm me down.

"Here, take this." Isabella seemed to have read my mind. I inhaled the vape she handed me and felt my body decline into relaxation. We headed to my bedroom where Izzy instructed me to sit on the bed while she rummaged in the medicine cabinet for an antiseptic rub and plasters to clean and cover the small cut on my hand. Once she was done, she took a shower and climbed in bed with me.

"What are you thinking?" She whispered in my neck as she wrapped her arm around me.

"Why are our lives so fucked up?" She tightened her hold on me as tears fell down my cheeks. That was the first time I really crumbled and fell apart in front of Isabella. Izzy woke up at 7 a.m. the next morning and made pancakes for breakfast. I rolled over in bed to find Mathew standing by the door.

"Get the fuck out of here!" I jumped out of bed with readiness to force him out the door.

"Let me explain. Please."

"There is nothing to explain. You lied, and it seems you've been lying and fucking someone else the entire time we got back together!" I was enraged.

"Well look at the pot calling the kettle black. You've done the same thing to me."

"I apologised for what I did. I told you why, and we were working to move forward. I didn't go out of my way to lie to you, and I've been honest about Lars.

We're not doing this anymore, just leave, please. Take all your things and get out." My ears were ringing.

He went into the bedroom, grabbed his bag and left. Isabella came over and hugged me. We looked ridiculous in an embrace. I was tall and muscular, and she tiptoed to reach as she was tiny. I was grateful to have her there. We finished breakfast and lounged on the sofa. Isabella caught up with work emails and her blogs as I flicked through TV channels to find something to watch. I needed to take my mind off the debacle of my life. It was approaching 10 a.m. when the doorbell rang multiple times. Izzy went to answer as I readied myself for another argument with Mathew. I mumbled profanities as she sashayed towards the corridor.

"Oh my god." I rushed to see what had happened and was immediately alert and concerned. Ryan was standing in the hallway with his face covered in bruises and cuts. His T-shirt was stained with dirt and smidges of blood. Izzy quickly closed the door behind him.

"Call an ambulance!" Isabella shouted in panic.

"No, it looks worse than it feels. No one can know I'm here." Ryan whispered.

"Okay. Please help me get him to the sofa. I'll get him some codeine for the pain."

We managed to drag Ryan into the living room and propped him on the sofa. I took two codeine tablets from the cupboard and gave it to him with a glass of water. Izzy was standing over him with her eyes searching for answers.

"Don't question it now. Clean his cuts and let him sleep for a bit. We'll deal with it later."

"What has he gotten himself involved in Frank?" She bit her lip. I knew it was painful for her to see him like that, but there was nothing we could do. I shrugged and walked to the bathroom, emerging with the first aid box. It seemed that we were all pushed to scrap like children in the playground.

Izzy cleaned the cuts and placed a light blanket over Ryan. We migrated to the kitchen and made ourselves some coffee to process the situation.

"The cash is at home. If he needs it today, we'll have to go there together. I'm not walking around the city with a bag full of money on my own. I was going to ask you to come with me tomorrow anyway." I nodded.

"Do you think it was a bar fight or he got himself in some trouble?"

"This doesn't look like a bar fight. He said no one could know he's here. I don't know what's happened, but it's something I know I don't want to get involved in. We'll help him nurse himself until tomorrow or Sunday at the latest. I will give him the cash and do the transfer for the rest of the money, and he can be on his way." Her face was cold, and I understood why she needed to handle the situation like a business transaction. She had been through enough already and after seeing the state Ryan was in, I thought it was the right decision for him to leave.

"Now what?"

"We wait for him to wake up."

Ryan stirred himself awake just after lunchtime. Isabella and I were sitting in the kitchen when we heard movements in the living room.

"What did you give me?" He yawned.

"Codeine. You can have more, but first, we need to know what's happened before you fall back into slumber. He sat up and drank a glass of water.

"I told one of the guy's that I no longer need the credit cards and they didn't take it well. They demanded money for the hassle, and I refused to pay." Izzy looked at him intently.

"So now, you've potentially led them here." I spat.

"I haven't told anyone that I know you or where you live. Anyway, I won't be here for long." He looked at Izzy.

"I suppose you want your money then. The cash is at my apartment, and I'll need my laptop to transfer the rest."

He tried to stand up but fell back on the sofa and held his chest in pain. I gave him two more codeine tablets and watched as he faded into oblivion.

"Should we go now or?"

"No. We're not leaving him here alone in your apartment. We'll wait for him until he can walk, then we can all go."

We sat in silence for a moment.

"Do you trust him? I mean, what if he tries to kill you after you give him the money."

"The way I tried to kill him?" She laughed. "Then I'll deal with it when it comes."

Isabella

Ryan woke up at 3.30 p.m. to have a shower. Frank helped him to the bathroom, where I helped him to undress. My heart raced when the bruises revealed themselves on his chest and back. He winced when the hot water touched his skin.

"You don't have to stay and watch. I'll call out when I'm finished." His voice echoed from the shower walls.

"Are you planning to kill me when I give you the cash?"

There was a pause, and my heart rate picked up as I prepared my ears to hear the answer.

"We had a plan for me to leave the country. Yes, the thought of killing you had crossed my mind, and I've been vocal about it, but as you can see, my body is battered. I wouldn't have it in me to do that even if I still wanted to." He exhaled.

"Okay. I guess there's nothing else I need to say."

I walked to the kitchen and saw Frank had made sandwiches. I plated two slices and started eating. Ryan called out for Frank to help him walk back to the sofa, where I brought him a plate with a few slices.

"The cab is here." We made our way out with Ryan leaning on Frank's shoulder for support. The cab journey back to my apartment was suspiciously quiet, and I wouldn't have blamed the driver for assuming we were undercover criminals because we were. However, I gave a generous tip that made his day. Once in my apartment, Ryan rested on the sofa while Frank sat at the dining table. I walked straight to my bedroom and opened the drawer that was locked in my closet. The bag contained money rolls, twenty-five thousand pounds that I had accumulated in the last few months in case I needed to leave at short notice. I wasn't worried about giving it to Ryan as I had more in stocks and some cash in savings. I walked to the living room and handed him the bag to check.

"It's all there." I grabbed my laptop. "I need your account details for the wire transfer."

He confirmed the details, and I transferred the rest of the money. It was done.

"So, what will you do now?" Frank asked the question that swirled in my head as Ryan winced in pain.

"Call me a cab to the hotel please."

Frank called me over to him for a word.

"We can't let him leave like this. What if those people follow him and steal the money? He can stay here with you." I quietly protested. The last thing I needed was for Ryan to get into more trouble and lose the cash, but I also knew how difficult it was going to be having him there.

"He has no one else, Izzy. We've all fucked up and at least this way you can keep an eye on him until he leaves. Keep something by your bed in case he tries to kill you while you sleep." Frank teased, but I was unable to find humour in his words.

"Right. You're staying here with me until you're better. You can't just hop in a cab across the city with a bag of cash if these people are looking for you."

"I'll be fine." Ryan tried to protest.

"No, you're in pain and need to rest without worrying about people breaking into your room." Frank interrupted and handed him two more painkillers. "Don't worry, they're from the pharmacy. Save the strong stuff for tonight."

Frank helped me set up the blow-up bed that I've never used, in the corner of the living room, obsessing over fluffing the pillows and ensuring the sheets and duvet cover matched. As if I had ever purchased mismatching linens. We all danced around awkward pleasantries for a while until Frank announced he was going home. Anxiety crept through my chest as I realised that Ryan could potentially be crashing in my apartment for longer than the weekend. I went to the bedroom to catch my breath while he laid on the sofa. He staggered over and knocked on the door.

"Are you okay?"

"Yes, just need a minute to freshen up."

I came out and busied myself with laundry and eventually sat at the dining table with my laptop to rearrange my calendar for the following week. Fortunately, I only had two clients booked, and they always understood my ever-changing circumstances.

Chapter Nine

Isabella

Ryan slept for the rest of the afternoon, and I occupied myself in the kitchen. I decided to cook grilled salmon, lean greens and homemade soup. It was a safe choice in case Ryan couldn't stomach the salmon. I was busy enjoying myself listening to music through my headphones while preparing the greens and marinating the salmon that I didn't notice Ryan watching me.

"God! You scared me."

"Sorry, you looked like you were having a great time. What are you listening to?"

"Ibiza classics." I smiled.

"Nice. Good for a gym playlist."

We stared at each other awkwardly before he slowly took a seat at the island. I carried on with the marinating and tossed the fish in the oven.

"How are you feeling?"

"Better." He fixed his eyes to the floor.

"Don't lie to me." I leaned on the island and dared him to look at me.

"Fine. I'm in clip." He chuckled to himself, but I remained quiet. He took two more painkillers and slowly went back to sit on the sofa. I followed.

"I have to be honest with you. This has caught me off guard, and I'm finding it difficult to see you like this."

"It wasn't my idea to stay here. I can leave."

"No. You're staying here for as long as you need. It will be difficult at first, and I'm sure you feel out of place, but we'll adjust. I'll be working on my blogs, and you can watch whatever you want. I can ask Frank to bring over your things from the hotel. That way, you don't have to go back there when you're ready to leave." He gave me a peculiar look that faded into a nod.

"Okay, thank you for your generosity."

The oven clock went off just as my stomach started to grumble. I served dinner, and Ryan inhaled his food within ten minutes. I cleared the plates and started the dishwasher while he switched on the news. I served myself a glass of wine and sat in the armchair next to the sofa.

"None for me?" He grinned.

"I don't think that's wise. You still have codeine in your system."

"A glass won't hurt. I know my limit, Izzy."

I served him a glass and relaxed. We didn't talk much, but it felt comfortable to sit and enjoy the moment. Before we knew it, the sun was setting, and Ryan fell asleep.

My alarm went off at 7 a.m., which was very early for me on a Saturday, but I wanted to take the time to go for a run. I opened my eyes to see my living room ceiling reflecting itself. Ryan stirred. I fell asleep next to him and was mildly embarrassed at the situation, but it felt good to absorb his warmth.

"Hey, what time is it?"

"7 a.m. I'm going for a run." I prompted myself off the sofa, but he grabbed me into his arm, it felt too lovely and too real, so I wiggled my way out and went into the bathroom.

My heart was racing, and my desire for him was awakened. I quickly brushed my teeth, changed into running clothes and took a few deep breaths to steady my focus. When I came out, Ryan was making coffee. He looked good in my kitchen. I took a few sips and made my way to the park. I had to balance my mind. The running route I chose was much longer than usual as I was in no rush to go back to my apartment. My headphones vibrated with upbeat music, and I bounced through my first few steps to warm up. My feet quickly picked up the pace as the dark cloud from my problems disintegrated. Droplets of rain slithered down my forehead halfway through the workout, and I welcomed it. Suddenly, a woman came running towards me.

"Izzy? Oh my god, hi!" My heart was beating fast, and I couldn't tell if it was because of seeing Juliana or from my workout, however, the feeling that agitated my stomach wasn't from running.

"Juliana, hi. Long-time no see."

"I just moved in the area. I thought I'd go for a walk and map my way around."

Juliana and I met at a spa over a year ago when the Andrew and John situation started. At first, I thought our acquaintance was one of coincidence but, she later confirmed that she had some trouble with Andrew which, in all honesty, may have caused a domino effect with his thirst for fucking up other people's lives. Ryan had confirmed his friendship with Juliana, and although her and I had a rapport, she wasn't someone that I tried to see. I must confirm that right at that moment, I still wasn't sure if she had a role to play with the Ryan situation.

"Nice. Where about did you move? We can have dinner sometime and catch up." It was a date I wasn't excited about keeping.

"Just last week. Sure, I have your number. I'll text you the address." We engaged in mundane chatter for a few more minutes before we both carried on with our day.

By the time I arrived home, my hair and clothes were soaked. Ryan was in the bathroom, so I took the opportunity to have a look around the apartment, ensuring that everything was where it should. I walked to the bedroom where I deliberately left the door unlocked and checked my drawers and the safe. It was likely that Ryan had an adventurous look around, however, the lock on my secret closet and safe where impenetrable. I quickly changed into a bathrobe and sat on the bed as I waited for Ryan to finish up in the shower.

"Sorry, you should've shouted me out. How was your run?" He peaked his head in after he emerged from the bathroom.

"It's no bother. I'm not in a rush. Interesting. I bumped into Juliana." His eyes widened with shock, but then he quickly gathered himself. However, I had already discerned what it was, and I didn't like it. He was up to something, and I had no doubt that she was in on it too, but I played along.

"Really? What did she say?" He walked in and sat on the bed.

"She just said she moved in the area last week."

"Oh, I didn't know she just moved."

"Really? You're friends, though." I got off the bed and made my way to the bathroom, leaving him to ponder on my comment as I didn't have the energy got the back and forth.

I grabbed my phone and locked the bathroom door to do some online searching in peace. Nothing on her social media accounts had indicated that Juliana had moved to Shoreditch. It was also weird that Ryan felt the need to mention that he did not know of this, considering his friendship with her. I immersed myself under the hot shower and began lathering my hair.

Buried thoughts of Andrew and John began to leak from my subconscious. It seemed that their ghosts would forever haunt my life no matter how much I emotionally and mentally tried to exorcise them from my experience. I conditioned my hair, and my curls instantly bounced into their volume. It had been a nightmare to maintain a straight hairstyle however, it was necessary to keep a low profile. Now that Ryan was in my flat with Juliana in tow somewhere in the area, I felt that I didn't have to hide too much anymore. I climbed out of the shower, towel-dried and moisturised every inch of my body and every strand of my hair. My mouth curved into a smile when I saw how sexy my highlights looked blended with my curls. I am now twenty-seven years old, and I still looked and felt like I was twenty-five: a blessing and a curse. I unlocked my phone and messaged Frank.

I MISS YOU, COME AND RESCUE ME. LOL

Miss you too! Omg, what's going on??

I bumped into Juliana on my run...I think Her and R are up to something.

Meet me at the café next to the boutique @ 10 a.m.

I agreed and walked to the bedroom to get dressed. When I walked in, Ryan was lying on the bed shirtless. My heartbeat rose, and heat crept up my spine. The bruises on his chest were fading, however, the muscles on his arms, shoulders and chest were not. He turned his head and smirked, inviting me to soak into his warmth. As tempted as I was, the thoughts in my head took priority, and I couldn't afford to be distracted although, I knew I had to pretend everything was normal or, as normal as our lives had been. I walked to the nightstand and showed him a tube of aloe vera.

"From now on, this is your best friend. It'll help your bruises fade faster."

"Okay. It'd be more fun if you helped me." He smirked.

I squeezed a generous amount in my hand and applied it to his back and chest while I tried to concentrate on something other than his bulging muscles. It was a lot easier to have sex with him when we both knew where we stood, and now, the line between wanting to kill each other and falling for each other was blurry. Not to mention the weird trivial energy between him and Juliana. We made conversation for a moment and then he announced he was going to rest on the sofa. I got dressed and proceeded to meet Frank for breakfast. The café was quiet, and I beamed with excitement when I saw Frank. Being with him was all I needed to extract my thoughts from the motion of Ryan's predicament. Frank had ordered eggs benedict for himself with a bowl of fruit. He looked put together in slim-fit trousers and a plain t-shirt. It was still the peak of the summer. I mimicked his look with cropped black trousers and a white t-shirt.

"It's such a simple pleasure to be out of that house." I said as I kissed his cheek.

"Oh, no. Aren't you getting on with the hunk?"

The waitress came over, and I ordered eggs royale with a smoothie. Saliva accumulated in my mouth as my stomach started to twist with hunger. I added a side of porridge with the order.

"It's so awkward. I thought we were growing into a better place, and I was getting used to having him around the house. But now Juliana is here, out of nowhere and he's pretending he didn't know."

The porridge and smoothie arrived quickly, and I fulfilled my obligation to eat. Frank patiently waited while I finished as he knew how whiny I got when hunger consumed me.

"Did you ask him about your suspicions?

"He would just lie. The man was thinking about killing me. Yes, we slept together, and there are feelings, but one of those feelings is resentment."
I grimaced before Frank could protest. The eggs royale arrived, and I started eating.

"Let's go out tonight. I'm so tired of this shit. I think we both need a break." I wasn't in the best place to go out, and I was sceptical about leaving Ryan alone in my apartment, but Frank was right. We both needed a break. I agreed.

"Have you heard from Mathew?"

"Yes, he keeps calling and leaving voicemails. I just can't bring myself to try and forgive him because he was so calculated. He got on his high and mighty moral sass horse when I fucked up, and he went out of his way to do the same. Anyway, it's done."

We finished our breakfast and talked about a few non-urgent matters. The catch up had alleviated our moods, so we decided to go shopping. As we walked into a boutique across the road from the café, my eyes were drawn to a mannequin that wore a mini dress. I asked the saleswoman for my size and tried it on.

"I love it, Frank! I'm wearing it tonight."

"Good." Frank smiled.

I paid for the dress and Frank confirmed we would have dinner at *Choux* and see where to go from there. I left Frank shortly after and made my way home. I messaged Juliana an invitation. When I arrived home, Ryan was asleep on the sofa. The bruise on his face was starting to fade, but, the cut above his eyebrow was still prominent. Frank had kindly brought the rest of his things from the hotel that piled neatly in the corner. The twenty-six-year-old me would've leapt at the opportunity to go through his things, but the twenty-seven-year-old me was now stealthy and careful.

I thought tonight was just us two. Why did you invite Dirty J?

Frank responded to my message. I knew he wouldn't be too thrilled, and I intended to indulge his company, but the Ryan situation wasn't going away. People kept coming back to haunt me. For as long as I was the linchpin holding this shitshow together, I had to keep plotting.

Dirty J, lol I know but we're gonna get her fucked up to get her talking. Then sling her in a cab home. ;)

Fine! You're paying for my drinks and my weed.

I can do better than that. I'm buying you dinner and something better than weed. x

Because I'm worth it. X

Frank had finally gotten me excited about our night out. It had been a while since I let my hair down, and I was determined to take care of business and have fun. I pulled my eyes away from my phone screen to see Ryan staring at me.

"You're in a good mood. How was breakfast?"

"Delicious! I'm going out tonight. You can order a takeaway, not sure when I'll be back."

He diverted his gaze to the floor, then readjusted his stance.

"Okay. Well, I'll be here watching a movie." He was bothered.

"Cool." I made my way to the bedroom and closed the door. My chest collapsed in a heavy exhale. My blood started to boil with irritation. The situation closed in on me, and I needed a release. I needed answers, but most importantly, I needed him to hold me and tell me that he loved me and wanted us to work this out. Before I knew it, I was in the living room with my finger pointed at him.

"This is my apartment and if I want to go out with my friend, or with anyone, I'm going to do so!" My abruptness caught him by surprise.

"Yes, you've made it clear it's your apartment and your life. I never wanted to stay here. Why are you even annoyed right now?" He erupted. He was right. I had created an issue in my head, and I just wanted to pick a fight rather than ask what the deal was with Juliana.

"I feel like you're lying to me! I don't hear from Juliana in nearly a year, and now all in sudden she's moved in down the road right at the same time you're here."

He froze for a moment, and I thought I saw his face change to admit that something was going on, but he didn't. "You're being ridiculous!" He walked to fetch his wallet and made his way to the door.

"Where are you going? Those guys could still be after you."

"I'd rather take my chances than stay another minute here with Lilith's offspring!" He slammed the door shut as he exited the apartment. I packed a small bag and got a cab to Frank's.

Frank

After breakfast, I came home and had a nap. I must have been asleep for an hour when the doorbell rang, and Isabella strolled into the corridor just as I opened the door. Her nostrils flared, and I immediately knew she had gotten into an argument with Ryan. My mind was disoriented from my nap, and my neck slightly ached. We walked to the bedroom where she placed her bag on the floor, and she climbed into bed with me. This was an act I was accustomed to when we both needed comfort. It was around 2 p.m., and we both slipped into slumber. We awoke at 5 p.m., and both of our moods were uplifted.

"What's he done then?"

"Nothing. I told him about us going out tonight, and he gave me a look. But in all honesty, I'm tired of this uneasy feeling whenever my thoughts go to him and Juliana. Something's off. Anyway, he stormed out and called me Lilith's offspring."

"How rude, you're Lilith incarnated." Frank chuckled.

"I had to get out of there. I need to breathe."

"But what if you're wrong about them? I spoke to him, and he said they're just friends. And from his story about Andrew, he does sound like a genuinely nice guy who helped his friend."

I understood and reasoned the situation, however, when it came to Izzy's life, I knew she was hardly ever wrong. We decided to leave things as they were and got ready for dinner at *Choux*. The dress she purchased from the boutique looked even better paired with studded sandals moreover, her hair and chic makeup emphasised her features. I wore a classic shirt, skinny jeans and a pair of high-end Chelsea boots. My hair was freshly trimmed, and my muscles were taut as ever. She grabbed my bag and took out a small container with two pills and handed it to me.

"You got me ecstasy?" My eyes lit with excitement.

"Yes but remember to start with half the pill. We don't need a situation tonight." We both laughed.

I tucked the container in my pocket, and we made our way to the restaurant. Izzy booked us the nicest table available, and we waited for Juliana to arrive. Her goal was to get Juliana drunk and sloppy with information as quickly as possible. Izzy ordered a bottle of Chateauneuf-du-Pape and beamed.

"I disapprove of you wasting this bottle of wine to get her wasted." I rolled my eyes.

"Who said she's drinking it all?" She smirked.

The waitress brought the bottle and served three glasses along with some appetisers. Juliana arrived and greeted us with a chirpy smile.

"Hi, darling, nice to see you again. This is my friend Frank." Izzy presented.

"Nice to meet you." I kissed her cheeks and smiled.

Juliana didn't hesitate to start sipping her wine, and we nibble the appetisers. Isabella and I deliberately took small sips as we waited for her decline. She excused herself for the bathroom just after we ordered the starters. Izzy discreetly pulled a small lipstick from her bag and pinched a small amount of codeine powder in her glass as soon as she disappeared from the foyer. Moments later, our starters arrived, and so did Juliana. We indulged in conversation about work and hobbies. Isabella's eyes sparkled with satisfaction each time Juliana's lips met with her wine glass. The powder began to work twenty minutes later as her body relaxed, and her speech slowed. Izzy asked her cryptic questions about her love life, and she confirmed she was single. Then she asked why she moved to Shoreditch, and she confirmed that her business wasn't performing well; therefore, her focus was to find new clients since the area was up and coming. We concluded it was time to leave upon finishing our main course. Isabella paid the bill, and even though it was frowned upon, I sweet-talked the waitress and took the bottle of wine with me. We got a cab and helped Juliana home. Isabella thought it was time we saw where she lived. By the time we got to her door, Juliana was woozy, and it was officially her bedtime. Her apartment was typical for a woman of her flair. Shabby chic and clean. Isabella tucked her into bed and placed a bottle of water on her nightstand. I occupied myself by checking the other rooms as Isabella managed to get her to unlock her phone. She wasn't worried that Juliana would remember the shenanigans in the morning because Isabella gave her just enough codeine to ensure she didn't. Besides, she did indulge on the wine. We checked her messages, emails and call history. There was nothing that indicated she was in contact with Ryan.

"Shit," Isabella muttered under her breath. It was time to leave. We rolled her on her side, Isabella placed her phone on the nightstand, turned the lights off and we left.

"Well, at least now, I know for sure." She said as we climbed into the cab.

"Indeed, time for my medicine." I giggled as I popped half of the ecstasy pill in my mouth and swallowed. Isabella placed the bottle of wine in her handbag. "Would you like some?"

"I do, but I'm going to be good tonight. It's all about you, so have fun, and I'll be here to ensure you keep having fun." She pinched my cheek. The cab took us to a club we had never been in before and since it was only 10 p.m. we didn't have to queue. We walked to the host and enquired if we could pay for a booth since we didn't have a reservation. To our luck, she escorted us to our table. We sat, and Isabella ordered a double bourbon for herself and a mocktail for me whilst the pill began to kick in.

"I'm feeling good!" I announced.

"I better level up then." She swallowed the bourbon in at once and ordered another.

The music picked up, and I resonated with everything that surrounded me. It had been a long time since I felt like the dark cloud of Mathew's disrespect lifted. I was in my happy place. Isabella drank her bourbons while I made conversation with beautiful men. We danced until sweat decorated our foreheads and it felt terrific to be carefree. At 2 a.m. we left the club and took a walk down the road for a pizza. We took a cab to my apartment, where my mood began to balance and devoured our pizza in the living room.

"Thanks for tonight, it's been fab!" I said as I chewed on my slice. Isabella opened the drawer in my nightstand and initiated an inhale on my vape.

"You're welcome, darling. I felt bad for invited Dirty J as you called her. I had to ensure you had a good time. I know it seems that everything has been about my mess lately, but it's not intentional. You're very dear to me, and I will always have your back. Always." Her eyes grew wide. "This will probably hit differently since I've had a few drinks but fuck it." She laughed.

We had the best end to an almost perfect day. Her suspicions about Juliana was at bay, and we could both focus on moving forward as soon as Ryan healed and left. As much as I had hoped they would work things out and blossom into something more than lies and crime, we both knew that she was better off without him. Ryan was nothing more than a beautiful man with baggage. We giggled into the early hours of the morning and fell asleep. The next morning, I awoke in the worst mood I could ever have imagined. It was 10 a.m., and I felt like my body could use with a few more hours of sleep. Isabella was in the bathroom, humming her favourite song. I climbed out of bed and headed for the kitchen, where I made us some coffee and toast.

She walked out in a bathrobe with her hair wrapped in a towel.

"Sorry for the hassle but I don't eat bread. I'll make us some scrambled egg and granola yoghurt." I nodded.

She proceeded to make breakfast. And we nursed ourselves back to reality. Halfway through our breakfast, there was a loud knock on the door. We ceased eating and looked at each other in confusion. I wasn't expecting visitors.

"It's probably Ryan coming to take me back to prison since I didn't go home last night." She joked.

I walked to the door and looked through the peephole. My heart thumped, and my blood began to boil under my skin. I opened the door to see the man I beat up at *Bar Hugh*. Mathew's bit on the side.

"What the fuck are you doing here?"

"Hi, I'm Darrian. Mathew said he forgot to collect his watch. He's been calling, but you haven't picked up, so I decided to come and get it for him." The nerve on this man. I paused for a moment and noticed the scars on his face that had started to fade. I composed myself and told him to wait in the corridor while I fetched Mathew's watch from the bedroom. When I returned, I heard Darrian exchanging words with Izzy in the kitchen. I stood in the corridor to listen. Isabella was telling him how out of order it was for him to show up at my apartment, but he wouldn't relent.

"Here's the watch. It's time for you to leave." We both stared at him.

"I'll leave when I'm ready." It was the tone in his voice that pushed me over the edge. I blacked out for a moment, and when I came around, Isabella was pressing a cold flannel on my forehead, like a mother soothing her baby. My head was ringing, and my neck was sore. The room was silent, and I felt my body shake as I looked around. Darrian was lying face down on my kitchen floor. Isabella's face was calm. It was the calmest state I had ever seen her in, and I felt the anxiety that creep up my spine.

"Oh my god. What did I do?"

"You fucked him up, that's what you did" She snickered, but I didn't find the situation amusing.
I got up and checked his pulse.

"He's dead. Fuck!" My vision was blurry, and my heart was racing. Sure, I had gotten into fights throughout my life, but I had never killed someone. The knot in my stomach tightened.

"Look it's always messy the first time but now's not the time to lose your shit. We need to get him out of here. You can lament the situation later." Logic would've prompted me to ask how Isabella could be so calm in the situation, however, considering her life experience, I would affirm that she was a professional. All in a sudden, a shock went through my body as the memory of the last ten minutes appeared. I saw myself from an external perspective and how quickly I lost my temper as I lunged at Darrian and tackled him to the ground. Bloodstained the corner of my kitchen table as I saw the frozen image of him hitting his temple on the corner of my beloved glass table, twisting his neck and tumbling to the ground. Just as I was about to call the guys, my front door opened, and Ryan uninvitedly walked through the kitchen to confront Isabella.

"I can't believe you drugged Juliana!" We all froze in apprehension.

"How the fuck did you get in my house?"

"The door was unlocked." He turned around and saw Darrian's lifeless body on the floor. "What is going on here? Who is he? Oh my god, is he dead?"

"He spontaneously came in, like yourself. Started giving us trouble so Frank tackled him to the floor, and he hit his head. Technically, it was an accident." He swallowed hard and looked at Izzy as though her tremendous calm for the situation alarmed him. He exhaled a heavy sigh, and I felt terrible to have him witness the snowballing mess of our lives, but at the same time, it served him right for walking into my house unannounced.

"We clearly can't call the police. We must get rid of him and his phone. Although, he must've told someone he was coming here." Ryan was right, but I didn't have the energy to showcase my agreement with Isabella's excitement. Darrian would've told Mathew he was coming to collect the watch however; I knew there was a slight chance that he felt the need to come around and gloat in supremacy without Mathew's knowledge. I decided to call the guys who helped Izzy and me with the Andrew situation. I checked Darrian's phone, and fortunately, it only required a thumbprint to unlock. I swiped the screen with his thumb and went through his call log and messages. Nothing indicated that Mathew was aware of his visit. His call log was quite dry. The guys arrived within ten minutes with their cardboard boxes. The situation was now costing my nerve and secret cash stash a fortune. I paid them in cash, no questions asked. I instructed them to have his phone wiped and incinerated as quickly as possible.

"Come on, boss, this is not our first time." They said as they wheeled Darrian's body out of my apartment. I walked and slumped on the sofa just as Izzy and Ryan began their bickering about why we drugged Juliana on our night out.

"You had no right to do that! Juliana is just a friend. You are crazy." Ryan exclaimed.

"You ain't seen nothing yet." Isabella smirked.

"Will you both just shut the fuck up! Another person has just died, and all you could think about is your egos. You lot might be accustomed to such situation, but I've never killed someone before, and I'm not doing so good. Yes, we took Juliana out last night but only because of you were acting shady Ryan, so of course, we needed to get to the bottom of it. And you, Izzy please for once in your life just admit why you're being crazy. Clearly, you're in love with him, and the thought of him being with Juliana drives you crazy hence the overreaction. You can both fight about this later but for now please, just shut the fuck up because my head hurts."

They both apologised and sat beside me on the sofa. Isabella patted my back while Ryan quietly murmured that we would be fine if we rode through the turbulent situation diligently. He reassured that Juliana had no part in the situation and she did not suspect that Isabella and I had drugged her.

"Honestly, she didn't even suspect anything. I decided to call her to see how she was settling in her new home. She mentioned she went out with you both and felt a bit weird and disoriented this morning. She didn't even remember how she got home, so I knew what the deal was. I swear to you Isabella, Juliana knows nothing. We are just friends." Ryan sighed. We sunk into the sofa, and silence consumed us.

Isabella

Frank decided to have a nap in his bedroom while Ryan and I drank some coffee in the kitchen. The air was thick with words we didn't know how to express, and Darrian's energy was still lingering, so I dug into my bag and lit a stick of Palo Santo to cleanse the space. It was the least I could do to help Frank get through this. I realised that as much as we held and defended each other, Frank still had a conscience whereas I, had already reached the point of no return. Yes, I meditated, ate well and looked after my health, but when it came down to the core of life's situations, I accepted that this was the life I had created and made for myself whether I liked it or not. This was my path, so nothing phased me.

"So, you're a shaman now?" Ryan grimaced.

"No, I'm the baddest bitch you've ever known." I snapped. "This is something to help cleanse the space for Frank. Although, I suspect he'd be moving soon."

We swirled in silence once more, but I took the opportunity to steal glances at him. I was still irritated with him but not because of Juliana. I believed what he said however, the fact that I couldn't allow myself to trust him made me feel powerless.

"I'm leaving by the end of next week." His words stung as they hit my ears. "I'm feeling stronger, and my body is healing well. I think it'll be best for everyone if I left."

"Have you decided where?"

"Devon. I need to be somewhere quiet and relaxed. Then I'll figure out my next move."

His voice was soothing. I had grown accustomed to having him in my apartment, and I wasn't looking forward to seeing him leave. I walked to him as he sat, hunched over holding his coffee cup where Frank's table once stood and pressed his head against my stomach. His hands grabbed the sides of my lower back, and we stood in this embrace while my guard faded away.

"Let's go home." My heart fluttered at the sound of him calling my apartment home. I ordered Frank some lunch to be delivered, checked he was okay and left.

Frank

I awoke just after 2 p.m. to the smell of Palo Santo. My legs were no longer wobbly, and my mind felt clearer. Isabella left a note indicating lunch would be delivered at 2.30 p.m., which was just on time as I was starving. My apartment was silent, my kitchen was spotless and looked bare without my dining table. The guys had removed everything incriminating. I considered redecorating, but I couldn't be bothered with the hassle, so I decided to start the hunt for a new apartment. A fresh start without Mathew and an attempt to bury the memory of Darrian's body lying lifelessly on my floor.

I've decided to move. Help find somewhere closer to you.

I messaged Izzy.

Done. X

I knew she wasn't surprised by my decision. We both had guts, but when it came to criminal activities, I drew the line at murder. My lunch was delivered, and I ate in deafening silence. I needed to blow off steam. I had a quick shower, got dressed and met up with Lars at Hotel Aldwych. When I arrived at the bar, he was sat nursing his whisky looking handsome as ever.

"Hey, it's been a minute how's it going?"

"Good, I'm glad you messaged me. How're things with Mathew?"

I paused and confirmed that things between Mathew and I was now over, and I was moving on. I acted as normal as possible as though the memory of the past few hours were nothing but a lucid dream. We sipped our drinks and talked for three hours. I wanted to do anything to avoid going home, but I decided that I couldn't get through this by avoiding responsibility. The only person I knew I could talk to was Isabella. She had given me a key for emergencies, and this was the case. I bought a bottle of bourbon and took a cab to her apartment. When I opened the door, I expected Ryan to be lounging on the sofa, but my face froze in semi embarrassment when I saw Isabella naked riding on him. Sex was not new to me, and I've had my fair share, but in my vulnerable state, I wished that I knocked or messaged her first. They both squealed in shock when they witnessed my frozen state. Ryan hurriedly wrapped himself with a blanket while Isabella sprinted to her bedroom.

"For fucks sake, Frank!" I silently walked to the kitchen and poured us all a drink.

"I'm sorry. You gave me a key for emergencies, and I needed to talk to you. I'll drink this and leave." I shouted across the room.

"No, you idiot! Don't leave." She emerged from the bedroom dressed in a kimono and made her way to the kitchen, where I held a tumbler out to her. She grabbed it and shot the elixir in one go. "Let's go sit on the balcony." I followed while Ryan headed for the bathroom. Isabella and I nursed the bottle of bourbon, and I spoke about how confused and blue I felt. She listened intently and empathised in a way that I didn't feel ashamed to expose my vulnerability. The sun was beginning to set when Ryan announced that he was cooking puttanesca for dinner. Isabella tried to hide her contentment, but I knew she was excited to have a man cook her dinner. We ate our spaghetti in silence which was more pleasant than awkward. An opportunity for us to internalise our life's debacles.

Chapter Ten

Frank

Before we knew it, Wednesday morning was upon us, and Ryan had lingered in Isabella's apartment while I managed to secure a new home in the building across the road from hers. I decided to upgrade and burrow myself in a two-bedroom loft. The building was colourful, but I was immediately sold on its private gym. Isabella had liaised with a few people to help me secure the lease exceptionally quickly and moving didn't take long since the loft was fully furnished. All I had to move was my wardrobe, toiletries and kitchen utensils. Isabella had been her patient and diligent self as usual throughout the entire moving process. As fabulous as she was, she helped to organise, pack and coordinated the move which took no more than three hours. Once in the apartment, we quickly unpacked and sighed with relief as it had already been cleaned. I walked through the open plan living room and giggled at the impeccable sight of my kitchen—all black with gold trims.

"This is amazing! Congratulations" she exhaled as she twirled around the room and struck a pose.

"Thanks for everything. You have some impressive administrative skills."

"Yeah, I know I'm such a blessing." She teased, although we both knew deep down that she was a blessing. We continued to mill around the loft, putting things in their respective places and collapsed on the sofa once we were finished. Isabella ordered some food and opened a good bottle of champagne. We sipped and chatted until the food arrived, quickly ruffling through containers dividing dishes because we were too lazy and hungry to care about using dishes. The lunch menu was Japanese, and we scoffed every morsel of it. We were talking about our household administrations when Isabella's phone rang. It was just after 2 p.m., and by this time, the champagne buzz had placed us in a fuzzy bubble of light-headedness with fizzing fingers. She was taking a while to reach across the coffee table, and I was too busy tucking into my dessert to help.

"Oh well, I'm sure they'll ring back," I said just before her phone vibrated multiple messages. We both giggled and dismissed it, teased that it was probably Ryan reminding her to pick up something from the shop. He had been there for a while, and despite their ups and downs, he had proven to be trustworthy. At this point, we were all just glad that Mathew hadn't found out yet. He hadn't called me, and for sure he didn't have reasons to show up at the apartment now that we had both moved on. Besides, he couldn't even if he wanted to anyway, I moved.

I finished chewing my dessert to find Isabella, stood frozen by the coffee table with her fingers gripped around her phone. At first, I thought that perhaps she was swooning over something naughty he had sent, but as I approached closer, something wasn't right. Her eyes glistened as she showed me a picture. There he was, and there were no doubts that it was Ryan, tied up to a chair in someone's living room with blood pouring down the side of his head. His eyes were swollen, making his face unrecognisable. Isabella snapped out of the shock and placed herself in logical fight zone.

"Fuck!" She grabbed her bag and made her way to the door. "Frank, I need you to stay here and don't contact me until I call you. This is not your fight, and I refuse to lose two people I love most in this world." I was too shocked and didn't have time to respond before she disappeared out of the door. Hearing her say she loved Ryan and me the most in this world was significant. Isabella, declaring her love for a man she slept with was significant indeed. I frowned at the fact that she told me what to do in this situation, but we would discuss that later.

Isabella

When Ryan's image opened on my phone, my heart knew that I had to help. I rushed out of Frank's loft to my apartment, where I carefully opened the door. Surprisingly, it hadn't been turned upside down like a burgle, there were no traces of blood or any signs of struggle. Everything was pristine, which meant they either grabbed him outside or visited him here and gave a choice to leave quietly. Just as I racked my brain for a map, my phone rang, and it was a private number.

"Yes." I answered confidently, but my knees were shaking.

"I'm sure you know what kind of call this is. We have just messaged an address to collect your boyfriend in exchange for fifty thousand pounds. You have two hours." The line went dead before I could respond. Shit. My phone vibrated and an address displayed on the screen. I checked it on the map, and it was a twenty-minute drive from my apartment. Fifty thousand pounds was doable but to move that kind of money around and withdraw within two hours was nearly impossible and I was running out of clients whom I hadn't already asked for favours. I went with my instincts to insist on transferring the funds from my offshore account. It wouldn't be easy, but I had handled far worse and was willing to take my chances. I walked to the bedroom and changed my clothes to something more practical but flirty. I opened the safe to check my treasures were still in place and swiftly secured the safe closed. I grabbed my work phone shoved it in my bag, walked to the cupboard and carefully placed the special bottle of bourbon I had infused with my special recipe in a gift bag. The bottle had been intricately resealed to look new. I knew the right measure I had to pour for the tipple to put someone to sleep, infused mild euphoria or stop their hearts. I had tested a small dose on myself, so I knew my limit. The situation was too risky to book a cab on my phone, so I decided to hail a taxi down the road. It wasn't an incredibly busy day, and I wouldn't say that I was lucky to grab a chap's attention, but I was happy that he was there swiftly. I swallowed slow, deep breaths as the driver weaved in and out of traffic and turned at each corner. The journey to less time than I thought, I exited the tax and handled him some notes and told him to keep the change. I looked up at the service apartments and immediately knew that the people who took Ryan were most likely high-class criminals, unlike the ones who loaned him the fake credit cards. The elevator took me to the third floor, and I quickly found the door I needed. 37. I knocked three times, and a pleasant-looking man opened the door. He didn't introduce himself, but I didn't mind considering I had no plans to forge a friendship with these people. He beckoned me to follow him, which I carefully did. Around the corner, in the living room, Ryan was still tied to the chair, barely conscious.

"This is not personal darling. His brother owed us a lot of money. This kind, hearted young man agreed to pay off the debt. I've been patient, but I don't have the time to play piggy in the middle with my money. We've been watching him for a while now, and he led us straight to you. You're emotionally involved on some level because he quietly agreed to come here so that we wouldn't hurt you." He smiled and continued as I watched him intently. "He's all yours, as long as you have my money. Otherwise, you'll both have a poetic death."

I narrowed my eyes and made a note of how many of them were there—just the three. I rationalised, I had to work my charm. "Well, it's insulting to assumed that I liked this man more than I loved money." They giggled. I casually held out my hand to hand him the gift bag. He shifted his gaze from me to his friend (which I'm quite sure was his lover) and back to me.

"I think we acquainted ourselves in such a grotesque manner here. I'm not a mobster, a thief or an assassin. Let's start from the beginning. You know my name is Isabella, it would be courteous of you to give me yours because whilst I do have your money, I would need your name to have it securely transferred to you. You didn't think I would be so silly to walk here with a wad of cash, did you?" I beamed. He blinked, and I resisted the urge to chuckle at his speechlessness. He checked the seal and gave me a puzzled look.

"I'm not here to kill you, and I couldn't even try anyway, don't be absurd. It's no hard feelings, I haven't had the best life, and I know I don't want someone like you on my back. I have the app to transfer your money, but we do need to wait for the agent to authorise and fast track the transaction. I thought we could have a drink while we wait."

I dismissed his response and took the bottle from his hand. Cracked it open and poured myself a small measure which I sipped with enjoyment. We all knew that he couldn't hurt me since the agent was essentially working for me and could abort the transaction if I didn't answer the phone to confirm what they needed. I thought that they could wait until after it was all done, but my mind hadn't gotten to that part yet. Richard, he confirmed his name and I flashed him my best smile. He took the bottle from my hand and poured him and his friends half a tumbler of the bourbon. I fiddled on my phone as I diligently sensed how much they had sipped. I talked him through the process and prompted him to add his details on the app. Between each time I pretended to savour a fake sip from my glass while the partners took long swigs of their drinks.

"Easy gentleman, it's a fine bourbon sip it like you deserve it." I smiled. They dismissed my comment. I looked over at Ryan, who was clinging on to dear life.

We waited for a few minutes before the agent called to go through the security questions which I was happy to confirm. "You will receive the final message with a code once it's done." I hung up and nodded. Deep down, though, I was enraged that they decided I was an easy target for this and the fact that Ryan kept a secret from me. I thought about leaving him to his faith and let nature take its course, but I knew that's not what my heart wanted. I had to push through anger and stay logical. The air between us grew thick with tension, but I'd be damned if I lost my cool. Richard's friends were slowly growing lethargic, and within three minutes, they had slumped into oblivion. Richard looked shocked and confused. He quickly stood up, but his legs crumbled and threw him hard on the ground.

"You bitch!" This phrase wasn't new to me. It took about five minutes for him to stop breathing. I called the agent to abort the transaction and to email the recipient's information to me for my safekeeping. I sensed there would be more worms like Richard to come along in the future, the information would be useful. I walked over and slapped Ryan awake. I was angry with him for putting me in this situation, but I was glad we were both still alive. I grabbed a knife and cut the ropes off him. His words slurred, but we managed to shuffle out of the building and hailed a taxi back to my apartment. Once inside, I checked his head, and the wound was now crusted with blood. His eyes were swollen and grooved with his forehead. I grabbed my phone and called Justin, one of my clients, who was a private doctor. He arrived within thirty minutes, checked Ryan's vitals, cleaned and dressed his wound.

"He's in a bad way, but he'll be okay. We need to keep an eye on his wound and make sure he's entirely comfortable. This will help with the pain and sleep. If he shows signs of a seizure, increased temperature and all that, go to A&E." I nodded at Justin's confidence and hoped Ryan remained stable as we were in no position to make ourselves vulnerable in a hospital. Justin patted me on my arm and exited my apartment. The clock presented its numerals as the sunlight dimmed on the horizon. It was just after 8 p.m. when I checked on Ryan. After I was sure he was okay, I peeled off my clothes and wrapped them in a plastic bag. It was good sense to dispose of them after my shower. I scrubbed and lathered my skin clean, patted dry and quickly moisturised. I changed in a pair of leggings, and a black T-shirt with my hair pulled back. Alarm rippled under my skin when I heard Ryan stir on the sofa. I hurried to the corridor, grabbed the bag and my keys and made my way outside finding the furthest bin available from my apartment. I dumped the bag in a refuse bin on a quiet street and walked back home, this time a little faster than before. Back in my apartment, I washed my hand and crawled in bed, exhausted. My mind was above anxiety at this point as I reasoned that Richard and his friends probably illegally own the apartments they used or perhaps even used a pseudonym to rent it. Either way, I was willing to deal with whatever came my way. The focus was to ensure Ryan was okay. I called Frank to let him know we were okay and reassured that the situation was handled. Soon after, my heavy eyelids fell close.

One Month Later

Ryan recovered quite well, and although he wasn't completely healthy, he had made himself busy plodding around my apartment. Some days he cooked, cleaned or bought the groceries. The space between us was filled with our longing and desire to protect each other, yet we were both skating on the edge of sanity. Some nights we made love in my bed and others we fucked on the living room floor. No matter how we spent time together, I dreaded the day he would leave, and I knew I didn't want him to. The day came quickly, and he had refused to take the fifty thousand pounds that I initially offered. He decided only to keep the twenty-five thousand he initially had with the argument that he could always make more money where he went. As for where he was going, he didn't disclose this information as he thought it was the best way to help us move on and avoid trouble. We stood on the station platform, my heart beating in my throat, and my head pounded with tension. I knew this day would come. It was a decision Ryan and I made and knew it was for the best. But standing there, looking into his eyes made me realise that it wasn't the best decision for me. I had gotten used to having him around, and in some way, he and Frank had become my family. Sure, our lives were messy, but it had developed and worked.

"I love you." It wasn't what I had planned to say. I knew that I loved him, but I never wanted to admit just how much I did. We had settled into each other, and at first, I thought it was nothing more than lust but saying it felt so natural and sincere. "The situation is fucked up, I know. But we can work something out. I don't want you to go. What we have is the most real and most unsettling passion I've ever felt in my life. I've tried to push it aside, and I know you feel the same way too." He had frozen into an unreadable state. It looked like he was rethinking his decision to leave. He cupped my cheek and placed his thumb on my bottom lip and leaned his forehead on mine.

"What we have is the most real thing I've ever felt. My heart aches for you Isabella, but I can't stay here. Too much has happened. We can't live our lives like this." Tears streamed down my cheeks as his words stabbed holes in my heart. I took a deep breath and closed my eyes to internalise the gravity of his words.

"Don't do this. Please." My vision was now blurry, and my eyes felt heavy. He kissed my lips hard and drew my body into his chest. We were so close that his warmth could melt my being down to nothing. He let me go as soon as the train arrived. He picked up his bag and walked to board the carriage. He didn't look back. I stood and hoped he would change his mind and come back, but he didn't. The train departed, and just like that, he had disappeared.

The End

Books by J.P. Mooney

tiny reads:
A poetry collection for on the go spirits

Isabella:
Crime has never looked this fabulous

Prana: Poems of the Moment

Virgo's Carousel:
Are you brave enough for the ride?

Mercury Retrograde Poems:
Climbing off the Ferris Wheel

Available on Amazon

www.ingramcontent.com/pod-product-compliance
Lightning Source LLC
Chambersburg PA
CBHW051847170626
46807CB00003B/1393